She'd never been this close to an actual vampire...

Between one breath and the next Raina found herself wedged against the wall with a hard male body too dangerously close to her own in front. Power, like smoke billowing from a forest fire, rolled off him in waves. As he pinned her with his arms on either side, the lethal look in his golden eyes was mesmerizing like a wild animal's.

With an audible *flick* his sharp fangs appeared out of the gums just above his very normal-looking teeth. His voice came out low, almost a growl. "I'm perfectly capable of doing anything you could possibly need done, Officer Ravenwing. But let's get one thing straight. You came to me. You need me. So if I tell you to jump when we're out there bushwhacking, you don't ask why, you just jump. I don't want to have to explain to my commander why I came back with a dead game warden. Are we clear?"

Books by Theresa Meyers

Harlequin Nocturne

The Truth about Vampires #107
The Vampire Who Loved Me #113
The Half-Breed Vampire #132

*Sons of Midnight

THERESA MEYERS

Raised by a bibliophile who turned the family dining room into a library, Theresa has always been a lover of books and stories. A writer first for newspapers, then for national magazines, she started her first novel in high school. In 2005 she was selected as one of eleven finalists in the nation for the American Title II contest, the *American Idol* of books. She is married to the first man she ever went on a real date with (to their high school prom). They currently live in a Victorian house on a mini farm in the Pacific Northwest with their children, a large assortment of animals and an out-of-control herb garden. You can find her online at her website, www.theresameyers.com, on Twitter at www.twitter.com/Theresa_Meyers, or on Facebook at www.facebook.com/TheresaMeyersAuthor.

THE HALF-BREED VAMPIRE

THERESA MEYERS

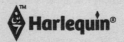

TORONTO NEW YORK LONDON
AMSTERDAM PARIS SYDNEY HAMBURG
STOCKHOLM ATHENS TOKYO MILAN MADRID
PRAGUE WARSAW BUDAPEST AUCKLAND

Recycling programs
for this product may
not exist in your area.

ISBN-13: 978-0-373-61879-8

THE HALF-BREED VAMPIRE

Dear Reader,

Welcome to the third story in my Sons of Midnight miniseries. When I first saw Slade Donovan he was a demolitions expert for the Cascade Vampire Clan security team in *The Vampire Who Loved Me*. I didn't realize at the time that his past was about to come back to bite him with a vengeance.

Raina Ravenwing is more wrapped up with Slade than even she realizes. And as she tries to balance the demands of her duties as a game warden with the needs of her tribe and what she considers to be their outdated, mystical ways, she learns that not everything, even the man she loves, is what it seems on the surface.

I played Lady Gaga's song "Monster" over and over as I wrote this book. I hope you enjoy this new addition to my stories in this series.

Warmest regards,

Theresa Meyers

For those we love,
no matter where they are and how things change.
For only the heart knows why we love.

This book is dedicated to my friends who love me
even though I'm sometimes a crazy writer:
Karla Baehr, Jennifer Hansen, Rachel Lee,
Kendra Lutovsky, Diana Burko and Dorina Potz.
You girls are the best.

To my dad, Ron Sauro, for being both a brilliant
scientist and a foolhardy romantic.

To Bonita Jay for being the best stepmom ever, and
loving my dad the way only you can.

And to Jerry, because even after twenty-five years
together, I still love you. Thanks for encouraging
my dreams.

Chapter 1

Something big and dark slipped into the shadows at the tree line, disappearing from view among the jagged rocks.

Slade Donovan lowered the throwing star he'd been prepared to let fly if the animal had moved any closer. It'd been too big for a coyote. Maybe a cougar? But it hadn't smelled like one. It had smelled...like wolf.

Overhead the crescent moon sliced through dark scudding clouds. Rain was coming in tonight on a cool wind. The scents of ocean and wet fir trees blew in gusts across the Puget Sound through Snoqualmie Pass, rustling Slade's dark hair with invisible fingers.

He pocketed the metal star and crouched into lurk mode. Two more hours and his shift would be over. He glanced back at the waxing moon. They'd already had one full moon this month. And, lucky him, there was another on its way.

The vamp doctors at Cascade Clan headquarters couldn't explain his moon sickness. Shaking sweats. Feeling like his skin was about to split into ribbons. An ache in his fangs so bad Slade had seriously contemplating having the bitches pulled, if growing them back in wouldn't have been just as painful.

Lots of agony, but no explanations.

It didn't help that he had nothing to go on as far as medical records or family history. His first memory had been of waking up in Seattle alone and terrified. For two years he roamed the streets. He'd been eightish they figured. The vampires of the Cascade Clan had taken him in and trained him as a Shyeld, until he was old enough to decide if he wanted to become one of them. He hadn't been too keen on finding out exactly how or why he'd been thrown away in the first place. He was more of a live-in-the-moment kind of guy.

Slade rolled his tight shoulders, the tension the moon brought out in him already coiling there. He forced himself to relax. He needed to think positively. The full moon would come and it would go. The pain and agony would pass, just like it always did.

He scanned the darkness for whatever had been lurking there a few minutes before, and wondered what kind of creature would be out here hunting in the woods. He was fortunate he didn't have the security team day shift. That one sucked. He'd done that a time or two and ended up with the mother of all migraines the next night and a sunburn he doubted he could have prevented even if he'd slathered on SPF one million. Working out in the sunlight wasn't fun when you were a vampire, but it could be done.

He was just grateful he had the night shift, which, hell, had its own problems.

Behind him the wind shifted for a moment. His nose filled with the scent of predator, wet dog, but more feral, and the odd scent of something sweet and feminine, close. A pack of whatever those creatures were was inching toward him from what had been downwind until a second ago.

As the hair on the back of his neck lifted in warning, he slid two fingers into his pocket and pulled out his throwing star.

A shadow darted through the base of the trees, followed quickly by two more. He heard their guttural growls and yips to one another, a language he could somehow understand, although he'd left that little tidbit out when talking to the clan doctors. Moon sickness was enough of an oddity among vampires. No need to be thought of as an even bigger freak.

"Think we can take the bloodsucker?"

A loud sniff. "There's only the one. Easy."

"But what if he's the one Bracken's been searching for?"

"Then all the better. We kill him now, quick and clean, before he can disrupt the pack."

The wind shifted again and the scents disappeared, but Slade readied himself, placing his weight on the balls of his feet so he could more easily spring at them when they got closer. Preparing for their attack, he pinched the throwing star between his fingers.

They vaulted forward through the underbrush, loping toward him with deliberate intent. Slade only had a moment to leap upward into the trees as the wolves rushed in, converging on the spot he'd been hiding moments before.

No ordinary wolves. Larger. Stronger. Smarter. One lunged, capturing Slade's pant leg between razor-sharp teeth, slicing clean through the denim. The wolf gave a vicious yank. Slade's one-handed grip on the tree branch overhead slipped at the unexpected force. He landed hard on his back and found a pair of paws the size of dinner plates on his chest, and a pair of feral brown eyes inches from his own.

The excruciating pain told him the weight of the beast had cracked his ribs. But the pain was the least of his problems as a snarling muzzle loomed over his face. A string of saliva stretched from the sharply pointed canines to the vicious-looking row of bottom teeth.

Slade shot out his hand, closing his fingers around the creature's thick neck and squeezed. The muscles in his arm bulged with the strain, and he felt as well as heard the deep-throated growl vibrating down his arm. He used all his strength to keep the animal from ripping out his throat.

It was a hell of a wolf, but just a wolf. Still no match for a vampire, he told himself mentally, even while his instincts told him differently.

Slade pulled his foot up between him and the beast and, with a grunt, kicked as hard as he could, launching the animal into the trunk of a massive fir tree. The loud crack of impact echoed like a gunshot through the woods. The wolf grunted, falling to the ground, stunned but not dead, then ran off into the trees.

What the hell?

He heard a sharp gasp and turned his gaze toward the sound. In the woods stood a woman, her mouth an open O, her face a pale full moon against the darkness of her hair and the night-shadowed woods around her.

He didn't have time to stare; two more wolves were on him like newborn vampires on a pint of A positive. He chucked the throwing star at one, hitting it in the eye. It yelped and sagged to the ground, its sides heaving. The woman screamed. The other wolf jumped up and over Slade, slapping him hard in the head with a paw that had the force of a baseball bat. As a chaser, the claws dug in, ripping flesh in a white-hot burn.

Ichor, black and thin, poured from the gash on his scalp and ran down his temple. Slade ignored the throbbing pain and wiped away the warm viscous fluid seeping into his left eye. The wolf had landed quickly and spun around, standing his ground, feet spread wide in the damp detritus of brown pine needles and crumbled stone on the ground. A ridge of dark gray fur encircled the large wolf's neck and stood up along its back. Bared teeth gleamed white in the moonlight filtering through the trees. A low, threatening rumble reverberated in the animal's deep chest.

Slade moved into the stance of a defensive linebacker, placing himself between the wolf and the woman, and answered with a low, feral growl of his

own. For a second the wolf's flattened ears raised a
fraction, then pinned back harder against its head. The
wolf eyed him warily, its great brown eyes piercing in
the darkness. The growl reformed, slurring and warp-
ing into actual words.

"Stay away from our border. Next time there will be
no warning."

All the tension in Slade's legs suddenly gave way,
making him stumble back a step. These weren't wolves
at all. They were damn shape-shifters—Weres. No
wonder he could understand them, no wonder they were
so huge. If this was a warning, he sure as hell would
hate to get a full-out war going with these things without backup.

The gray wolf retreated slowly, gaze locked on
Slade's, his hackles still raised until he reached the
darkness of the trees. And then, like a nightmare, he
was gone.

Slade sank to his knees, his arm wrapping around
his broken ribs. They seared and burned as they began
to knit back together. Thank the gods he didn't need to
breathe. Chances were the ribs had pierced his lungs,
but they were functionally useless, so it wouldn't kill
him, just hurt like hell. He touched the gash on his head
and glanced up to look at the woman.

She was twenty-five feet away, kneeling by the
downed Were. Her doelike brown eyes were just a
shade too wide and bright over the flushed prominent
cheekbones the color of dark honey. Her gaze darted
around her surroundings. Like a deer, she was small,
lithe, with delicate wrists and shoulders softened by

the sunny yellow fleece zip-up jacket she wore. Soft faded denim hugged her legs and the curves of her ass and she wore small muddy hiking books. Slung over her shoulder was a worn backpack.

She smelled of sunshine, wood smoke and strawberries. His preternaturally sharp sense of smell was even more attuned than most vampires. A possible side effect of the moon sickness, he'd been told. In the past twenty-four hours she'd walked past a mossy stream bank, the wet earthy scent of it still clinging to her shoes. She'd pushed past cedar and fir and huckleberry. Traces of it lingered around her like notes of an expensive perfume. Underneath it all was clean female skin.

Delectable smells notwithstanding, she was definitely not his type. Not even close. He preferred his women polished and professional, citified and slick. She had nature girl written all over her. And frankly he'd had enough of the great outdoors for one night. Besides, what the hell was she doing out here in the middle of the night, anyway?

"Are you hurt?" he asked, and took a single step in her direction.

Those big brown eyes turned his way, dark with fierce anger. "You killed him." Accusation gave her softly spoken words the edge of a razor.

"Did they hurt you?"

She shook her head. Her hair, mussed with bits of dried needles and twigs, floated about her head like a dark cloud with the movement. "I was following them."

Slade narrowed his eyes. "Why are you out here?"

She pinned him with a glare and reached for the

small of her back, pulling out a 9 mm Glock. "I might ask you the same. Do you always hunt on protected state land?"

Slade put his hands up in self-defense and blinked back the dribble of ichor seeping into the corner of his eye. "Whoa. Hold up there, lady. I just saved your life."

She stood, bracing her feet wide apart in a practiced shooting stance, both hands firmly on her weapon. "No, what you did was kill an incredibly rare wolf. I've been tracking this pack for months. I finally actually get to see them and then you have to go all cowboy on me and kill one and chase the others away. Are you aware killing a wolf is a crime, sir? You are under arrest."

Slade bit back a laugh. Under arrest? She had to be kidding. He was a trained Shyeld, and outweighed her by fifty pounds, all of it muscle. "Who are you?" he asked, scanning the woods behind her for any sign of the pack.

"Game Warden." She reached for her back pocket with one hand and pulled out a plastic zip tie. "You have the right—"

She cut off her reading of his rights with a loud scream. Behind her erupted a flare of brilliant light as fire engulfed the fallen wolf's body. Slade yanked her toward him to keep her from getting singed by the blaze. She smacked up against his chest, all soft curves, then twisted back, holding up her hand to shield her face. A cry of shock and anguish escaped her and she turned, gazing up into his face. "What happened? Why did it spontaneously combust? What did you do?"

Slade gave a heavy sigh and took the opportunity to

relieve her of her gun. She was asking too many questions. Mortals might know vampires existed, but they knew nothing of Weres. And he wasn't about to be the one who broke that bad news to them. He gazed deeply into her eyes, focusing on wiping him, the wolf, and everything that had just happened from her mind.

"This is all just a very vivid dream. You've been working too hard," he said slowly and deliberately.

Her confused gaze softened, turning hazy and unfocused. Her furrowed brow smoothed as the glamour he'd cast took over.

"Vivid dream," she echoed back. "Work too hard." Her eyelashes fluttered and she began to slump to the forest floor.

He caught her before she hit the leaf litter and swung her up into his arms, his barely healed broken ribs protesting with a fiery shot of pain. Slade grunted. She was totally out and heavier than she looked. He'd never had a glamour work so well before.

"Let's find out where you parked," he murmured to the darkness. He began trudging through the trees, the unconscious woman in his arms. He sniffed at the air, following the faint trail of strawberries and gunpowder she'd left behind as she'd walked through the woods.

It took a half hour but he found her car, a white compact vehicle, parked alongside the highway that wound through the mountain pass. He shifted her weight and tried with one hand to open the door. Locked. Damn.

"Lady, you're a whole lot more trouble than you look," he muttered. He mentally clicked the locks open and settled her into the backseat of her car, gun on the floor, arranging her so she would think she'd just fallen asleep in the backseat when the glamour wore off.

Dawn was starting to creep along the horizon, reaching out stealthy fingers over the peaks of the Cascades. Slade straightened, wiping away the dribble of ichor seeping down the side of his face. Time to pack it in and call it a night. Good thing he could sleep the next twelve hours. He needed it.

He took one last look at the woman, her chest rising and falling in the soft rhythm of sleep. "It was nice to meet you, Officer," he said under his breath, "but here's hoping we never meet again." He shut the car door and vanished into the night.

Chapter 2

Total bliss only lasted four hours.

Hey, Donovan. You got a visitor. The voice of his commander, Achilles Stefanos, echoed in his head, waking him from a dead sleep and leaving his ears ringing.

Slade grimaced, turned over in his tangled sheets. *Talk about lousy timing. Can it wait?*

No. Get your ass in here.

What vampire on Earth would want to speak to him at this ungodly hour? Either something was wrong, or was going to be. Slade grumbled. He grappled the sides of his sleeping spot, a double-wide grave-size hole carved out of the gray bedrock, the black satin sheets pooling around his hips as he sat up.

He phased himself a fresh-showered look and clean

fatigues so he'd at least appear presentable, then focused on gathering his energy together at his core, visualizing the security room inside the clan headquarters, so he could transport.

An image of pale green smooth walls and military-issue furniture circa 1950 filled his mind, accented by the musty smell that pervaded the room despite the heat thrown off by the banks of flat-screen computers. A pull, centered at his navel, yanked him inside out as he transported from his position in the Cascade Mountains to the complex system of passages and rooms fifty feet below the asphalt streets and buildings of Seattle.

The minute his particles knit back together he could see exactly why the hour was so damn late, or rather so damn early. His visitor wasn't a vampire. It was the woman from the woods, only now she was in full uniform for a state police officer—a pair of olive-green pants, a short-sleeved khaki shirt with matching olive-green breast pocket flaps and epaulets, a standard-issue gun belt, ugly black shoes and her glorious ebony hair pulled back in a no-nonsense bun at her nape. Damn. Double Damn. The cop.

Before being brought into the clan, he'd had his share of run-ins with the law and still felt uncomfortable around cops. Even pretty, strawberry-scented ones. He glanced at Achilles. His commander was one-hundred-percent pure golden Spartan warrior, but his modern military-short hair cut was starting to grow out. His hard jaw didn't flex in a smile, but the wicked twinkle in his unnaturally green eyes said he knew something about this woman Slade didn't.

Slade shifted, crossing his arms over his chest, forcing himself not to wince at the sharp sting in his ribs, which were still a little tender. "Can I help you?"

She extended a slender hand. Her nails were short and mostly clean; only a few had fine traces of dirt underneath.

"I'm Raina Ravenwing, Mr. Blackwolf," she said smoothly, extending her hand. There was no sign of recognition in her dark brown eyes. "Officer with the Washington Department of Fish and Wildlife," she clarified, just in case the emblem on her sleeve didn't do the job.

He stared at her hand but didn't take it, and she let it drop. "Sorry, wrong guy. Last name's Donovan. If that's it, I'm out of here." He turned on his heel, giving her his back as he headed for the door.

"So you go by your mother's maiden name?"

That stopped him cold. His mother's maiden name? He didn't know whose name it was, let alone why he'd used it for as long as he could remember. The only glimpse of his mother he'd had—at least he thought it was her —were in distorted, slow-motion images he saw in his daymares.

Dark hair, large brown-sugar eyes. A wide, generous mouth, which smiled one moment and screamed the next. A wash of red blood and the howl of wolves.

To think Officer Raina Ravenwing knew something about him that he didn't even know about himself rankled. He turned slowly, facing her once more. "Couldn't tell you. Don't know."

The petite woman widened her stance, pulled her

shoulders back and stiffened her spine. "Well, Mr. Donovan, I've been told you're a wolf expert of sorts." Her gaze flicked to Achilles briefly, disbelief evident in the firm set of her generous mouth.

The dark hair prickled all along Slade's arm. Somehow, gut deep, he knew she wasn't here to talk about just wolves. "I guess."

"Don't let him fool you, Officer Ravenwing. There's not another vampire who can track better than Donovan." It was true. Slade's senses were more finely tuned than most of the other vamps in the clan. That's why he'd been tapped to be in the security detail by the commander himself. While his technical specialty was explosives, tracking came in a close second. Very close.

She stuck her chin out a bit, almost daring him. "What do you know about unusually large wolves in our area?"

Slade brushed at the slowly healing cut at his scalp line. Good. She didn't remember a thing. Weres weren't something you talked about in polite vampire society, let alone with mortals. They were less than mortal. A cruel joke of the gods. A cross between an unpredictable animal and an unsympathetic mortal.

"Why?"

"There've been reports of some rather unusual wolves causing trouble along the edges of the Alpine Lakes Wilderness Area. The people are getting panicked by it and ready to go on a wolf hunt."

"So let them."

Her eyes narrowed. She crossed her arms over her chest, making her B-cup breasts jut out enticingly. At least he thought they were B cups. They might be just a shade larger, but he wouldn't be able to tell unless he got his hands on them.

Whoa. Where had that come from? Slade flexed his fingers, reining in his wayward thoughts. She wasn't even his type. Of course, who the hell did he think he was kidding? Female was his type. It was police officer that wasn't.

"My job as a Game Warden, Mr. Donovan, is to protect these animals and enforce the laws in this state. The fact that they've returned at all and may be migrants from the reestablished packs in Idaho or Montana is significant enough. They're an important part of our ecosystem and until I find out who or what is really behind these attacks, I'm doing my best not to let anyone near those wolves."

The scrape on his scalp was beginning to itch like holy hell and he wasn't really interested in her long-winded eco lecture. "Lady, the wolves aren't in any danger. If you want my advice, you'd do better to worry about keeping people away from them."

"It's Officer Ravenwing, Mr. Donovan, and that's about what I expected from a vampire." She said the last word with such disdain that Slade could smell the sulfur of it like rotten eggs tainting the air.

Achilles stepped closer, placing a huge hand on her delicate shoulder. "Officer Ravenwing, Donovan will be happy to help you with whatever you need to bring your investigation to a close."

Slade glared at his commander. *What the hell? I don't want to be anywhere near her.*

Achilles glanced back at him, his words echoing loud and clear in Slade's head. *She's part of the mortals' law enforcers, so we will cooperate fully. We don't need them digging up problems with the Wenatchee Were Pack. You'll help her or you'll be pulling day shift for the next decade. Do I make myself clear?*

Yes.

Yes, what?

Yes, sir.

Achilles gave the game warden a nod, and she relaxed. "If you'll excuse me, Officer Ravenwing, I have another pressing matter." He grasped her free hand and lightly brushed the back of it with a brief kiss. "I'll leave you to fill Donovan in on how you want this handled."

She gave Achilles a generous smile that pissed off Slade even more.

She blushed slightly. "Thanks for your help."

Achilles vanished in a swirl of dark particles as he transported from the room, leaving Slade alone with the cop.

He glared at Officer nature girl. Just because he had to help her didn't mean he had to like it. "What do you need?"

"I need your help tracking one of them down so I can find out if they've established a new pack from the groups farther east, or if they are a new breed or rare mutation. And find out what's really going on with this rash of incidents."

Damn. Double Damn. Sure, waltz in on the Were territory and give them a "hey, wazzup?" Why didn't she just ask him to go stake his balls to the ground and sunbathe nude? That would be less painful. Well, maybe. "So you want me to go on a nature hike with you?"

Raina restrained herself from making a smart-ass comeback. If nothing else she was a professional. She would have preferred to have Achilles go with her. At least he could be trusted and had some respect for her badge. With Donovan it was a whole other matter.

Everything about him shouted *danger,* from the rumble of his deep voice and dark good looks to his tigerlike topaz eyes. But it was the broad shoulders, encased in a tight black T-shirt, military-cut camo fatigues and a wide jaw bisected by a devil-may-care dent in his chin that were an even greater danger to any female in sight. That was, if he'd been her type. Which he wasn't.

Something at the edge of her mind nagged her. She'd seen him before. He'd done something horrible. But no matter how hard she concentrated, it floated in her memory just out of reach.

"It's a bit more complicated than that. There's an investigation currently going on. I need to track one down and put a locator on it."

He glanced away, sending not so subtle uninterested signals her way. "I'm sorry, am I boring you, Mr. Donovan?"

He shook his head. "Locator. Please continue."

Raina was slightly surprised he had actually been listening. "I need to know if there's only one, or if there are more and if so, what the pack's territory is so I can advise the State Department of Fish and Wildlife of the potential impact on local farmers and the game in the area."

She didn't like the way he narrowed his eyes. The air around him swirled with a potent mixture of testosterone and wild side that was too intense to be comfortable. While his commander was at least polite, Slade Blackwolf, or Donovan, or whatever he wanted to call himself, was barely civilized.

He reeked of bad boy, something she'd tried scrupulously to avoid since graduating the police academy. If she got close enough she could probably smell motorcycle fumes and leather on him if she tried. But she had no intention of getting that close, now or ever. Getting mixed up with a bad boy was career suicide for a cop, especially a young female cop, no matter what department she worked in.

This was business, plain and simple. Being a game warden offered her an opportunity to help out her tribe in a practical way instead of all the hocus-pocus they kept insisting she was somehow tied to as part of their hopelessly outdated beliefs.

From what she'd been able to discover, he was her best chance at finding the elusive wolves. So far everything else she'd tried had gotten her squat. And if things went on much longer it wouldn't be just the state she'd have to deal with; the Feds would get involved since her investigation was crisscrossing areas of the Wenatchee National Forest. She needed to find those wolves. Now.

"Sounds like a lost cause. Can't prove something's perfectly harmless when it's not."

Raina didn't like his belligerent attitude any more than his bad-boy demeanor. "Look, if you aren't capable of helping me—"

Between one breath and the next she found herself wedged up against the wall. A hard male body too dangerously close to her own in front and the rough edges of a cold brick wall digging into her back. Power, like smoke billowing from a forest fire, rolled off him in waves. He pinned her, his arms on either side, a lethal look in his golden eyes that was mesmerizing like a wild animal's. She'd never been this close to an actual vampire before and it scared the hell out of her.

With an audible *flick* his sharp fangs appeared out of the gums just above his very normal-looking teeth. His voice came out low, almost a growl. "I'm perfectly capable of doing anything you could possibly need done, Officer Ravenwing. But let's get one thing straight. You came to me. You need me. So if I tell you to jump when we're out there bushwhacking, you don't ask why, you just jump. I don't want have to explain to my commander why I came back with a dead game warden. Are we clear?"

Raina managed to gather enough moisture in her dry mouth to swallow, but words were beyond her. All she could manage was a nod, her heart pounding so hard her pulse throbbed in her fingers and toes.

All the resolve she'd made to keep far away from bad boys of any kind began to dissolve, running like heated honey through her veins. He was too close and it was too confining. She tried to push against him, her hands on his broad chest, and found herself falling forward and stumbling.

He'd dissolved beneath her touch into nothing but smoke, then reappeared on the other side of the room in less time than it had taken her to blink. His large hand was touching his chest where hers had been a moment before, his eyes darker than before.

His voice came out almost a growl. "Next time you touch me, it had better be because you want to."

Chapter 3

Raina swallowed hard, her slender throat, exposed by her upswept hair, flexing with the movement. Slade couldn't help fixating on the light, fast beat pulsing just beneath surface of her skin. Her heart beat loud and clear and the oceanlike roar of her quickly moving blood filled his sensitive ears.

The succulent smell of ripe strawberries suffused the air, making him certain the confection flowing through her veins would taste like strawberries on angel food cake. A real problem for him, since he had a serious sweet tooth.

Her eyes widened a fraction and she unconsciously slipped her hand up to her neck, cupping it over the spot where he'd been staring. "Look, Mr. Donovan, I think we may have started off on the wrong foot."

Slade snorted. They'd crossed that bridge a while ago out in the woods when she'd laid into him for killing that Were. Only one of them had forgotten it. Once he did, he'd forget that she was firmly on the side of the furries instead of him and his kind. "Doesn't matter. I'm not helping you to make friends. I'm in this because my commander gave me an order."

From the sudden rigidness of her frame he could tell the rebuff stung. Nature girl pulled back her shoulders, her full lips thinning slightly as she pressed them together. "Then perhaps we ought to get started."

Better to keep a distance between them than let the agitation that eddied like smoke in the air develop into anything more personal. He chose his next words to intentionally goad her. "Where to, babe?"

Her eyes turned hard, glittering, but she didn't take the bait. *"Officer Ravenwing,"* she reminded him sternly. "I think the most logical place for us to start would be where we received the first incident report with the wolves. We need to go to Teanachee. Know where that is?"

"Yeah." The hair on the back of Slade's neck rose like the hackles on a dog facing danger. Danger? What the hell? He'd never been to east of the Cascades unless he was on a plane.

"Cowboy country, huh? Missing Tex already, are you?"

She dismissed his gibe with a delicate little sniff, resting her hand on the butt of her holstered revolver and keeping her gaze level. "Ready to go, Mr. Donavan?"

Not in the middle of the day when he'd already been up all night. He didn't want to deal with a migraine from being in the light. Besides, he hadn't eaten since he went on shift, and starting off hungry with her blood smelling like dessert wasn't a good idea. He especially didn't like her thinking she could call all the shots. Slade crossed his arms. "What's your rush, Officer Ravenwing? Most shifters don't come out until dusk. We'll head out tonight."

Her smooth jawline tightened, and his extrasensitive hearing picked up the minute sounds of cracking enamel as she ground her teeth together. "I'd prefer to leave immediately. It's a two-hour drive, and there are things I'd like to look at while it's light."

He gave her a mock imitation of a grin and leaned his hip on Achilles's desk. "I don't feel like it."

"But your commander gave orders—"

"Which I fully intend to obey. But you might as well get used to the idea that vampires operate differently than you mortals."

She lowered her head, like a bull ready to charge. "I'm fully aware of the nocturnal habits of vampires, Mr. Donovan. But our quarry is nocturnal, too. If we aren't there to conduct our interviews and hike where we can observe them, our time today will be wasted."

Slade inhaled sharply, about to give her a piece of his mind, then found that breathing in around her was a mistake. Amplified by the small confines of the room, her seductive strawberry scent spiked with gunpowder filled his senses. There was nowhere to go for relief. He decided right then and there anything that got him

out of Officer Ravenwing's presence faster and back to
his normal duties would be a good thing.

The next best thing was being somewhere where
there was a lot of space, fresh air and other smells less
distracting.

"Fine. We'll do it your way. For now." He held out
a hand and materialized a packed black military-issue
duffel across his shoulder and back. A little gasp of surprise slipped past her full lips. Nature girl thought she
knew a lot, but clearly she didn't know everything. He
brushed past, her being careful not to touch any part of
her. "You never saw a vampire materialize something
before?"

With a frown, she shook her head slightly. "Just
where are you going, Mr. Donovan?" The asperity and
commanding tone in her voice rubbed him the wrong
way. Yep, the sooner he got good and gone from nature
girl the better off he'd be.

"Unless you want me to grab hold of you and transport us to your vehicle—" She gave an outraged little
gasp, but he plowed on. "Yeah. Thought so. Then I
suggest you start walking. Otherwise getting over the
mountains is going to take a while." He pulled open
the door and stalked out into the long brick labyrinth
of hallways comprising the Seattle Underground.

Her utilitarian boots clomped on the cement floor
behind him as she trotted to catch up. She might think
her under-her-breath growl of annoyance was too soft
to hear, but Slade had super hearing. For a moment her
irritation amused him.

"You don't even know where my car is parked."

Slade shrugged and slowed his steps so she could catch up. "I'm not the best tracker in the clan for nothing. I can find a car, no problemo." He leaned in close, taking a deep inhalation, making her squeak with indignation and step back a pace. "I'll just follow my nose." Of course, it didn't hurt that he knew the make, model and license plate. With that he spun on his booted heel and strode toward the parking complex several city blocks away to go find her car.

Of course, Office nature girl (or Strawberry Shortcake as he was beginning to think of her) insisted on driving. Slade didn't argue, just folded himself pretzel-style into the cramped front seat and pushed it as far back as it would go. It was still a tight fit for his long legs.

She asked politely what type of music he preferred as he turned on the radio, and when he said heavy metal, she tuned it to country because she didn't like his selection. Didn't bother him any. The music was loud enough to make casual chitchat impossible. He enjoyed the view of Officer Ravenwing and the passing scenery.

She was a competent, if cautious driver, and city streets quickly gave way to the tall, lush evergreen trees. An hour later he saw the rocky gray points of the Cascades topped with snow even in the late days of summer as the highway east wound through the pass through the Alpine Lakes Wilderness Area. As they started downhill, they jetted past the big reservoir that reflected the mountains and the brilliant blue sky dotted with white clouds. The land opened up, spreading out in swaths of first green, then golden grasses. The meadows were stuck here and there with frilly pines that became farther and farther apart. A couple hours' drive, and they were a world away from the bustling, crowded streets of Seattle.

The lay of land seemed oddly familiar. At least there were still trees, Slade thought. He shifted uncomfortably in his seat, making it squeak in protest. Normally, members of the clan never left the boundaries of their territory and this was hell and gone from the border.

"Almost there," she said as she flicked her gaze in his direction. "Teanachee is just up the highway from Cle Elum."

Goody. He could hardly wait.

They pulled off the wide strip of well-maintained asphalt that made up Highway 90 onto a far smaller, two-lane road that had seen better days. Slade's head hit the roof of the car as it bounced over car-eating potholes.

"We'll stop at Jake's before we head out to the farms that have been having the most trouble with these wolves."

Downtown Teanachee at rush hour consisted of one main street, an old-looking little gas and grocery jiffy mart named Jake's, a few shops, a few houses circa 1900-something and two cars, both parked at Jake's. If the forlorn town was sad, its backdrop was conversely majestic. The tall, imposing, purplish Cascade and Wenatchee mountain ranges colliding in points so high they reached into the clouds while their bases were fringed with a lacy skirt of evergreens.

They pulled into the quick mart parking lot and

Slade unfolded himself from the front seat and stretched.

"Man, how do you stay away?" he said just above a whisper as she got out of the car and strode past him. Even with those ugly pants on, Slade could tell that she had a nice firm butt and he'd bet Achilles a beer she had long slender legs to match.

The dark bun of her hair shifted over her shoulder as she turned to shoot him a glare. "May not be much to a big-city vamp like you, but for the people around here, it's home."

He didn't honestly have anything against small towns, except that they were, well, small. He'd never lived in one. The pine-scented air tickled his brain with an elusive memory, making him feel unaccountably edgy, as if he was anticipating a sneeze that never came.

A bell strung over the door of Jake's jangled an irritatingly cheery chime as they pushed into the minimart. Inside, the place was threadbare, but neat and clean, smelling of a mix of beef jerky, pickles and the hot, yeasty smell of fresh-baked bread. The combination of smells seemed achingly familiar, which was impossible. Slade shrugged off the misplaced sense of déjà vu and followed her to the counter.

An older woman with deeply tanned skin and hair as white and copious as wool on a sheep came bustling out of the back room. Her dark eyes lit up when she saw nature girl. "Raina! Come here. Give your auntie Mo a hug!"

The woman, who was nearly as wide as she was tall and dressed in a lurid red-and-purple muumuu, engulfed nature girl in a bone-crushing hug. "Now who is this fine young man you've got with you? A new boyfriend?" She chucked Raina under the chin affectionately with a crooked finger.

Slade stifled a smirk as Raina turned three shades of ever-increasing red beneath the dusky natural tone of her skin. She smoothed a strand of dark hair that had escaped her ruthless bun, tucking it deftly behind her ears. Apparently nature girl didn't get out much. Her gaze flicked in his direction for just a moment, but Slade was sure the temperature control in the small store was on the fritz because he could have sworn he'd gotten a blast of heat from her direction.

"No, just someone who's come to help us with the wolves that have been bothering the folks out near Red Top Mountain. We came in to grab a few supplies before heading out there."

The older woman wasn't intimidated, despite Slade's size. She strode straight up to him and looked him deeply in the eyes. Her pupils dilated some, a satisfied grin widening her brown cheeks further.

"Well, well, well. Look what the crow brought home to the nest." She put a pillow-soft plump hand, fragrant with the yeasty scent of warm bread, on either side of his face and pulled down until they were eye to eye. "Those are some unusual eyes you've got there, son. Same mouth. High cheeks and that devil's dimple on your chin. You must be Kaycee Blackwolf's boy." She patted his cheek affectionately, then waddled back behind the counter, the rubber soles of her shoes squeaking on the worn linoleum. "Can I get either of you children some jerky?"

"Who's Kaycee Blackwolf?" His question sounded abrupt even to his own ears, but a sudden uncomfortable churning had started in his gut and Slade didn't like it one bit. Not knowing about his past hadn't been too much of a hindrance among the vampires, but here, in the confines of the little minimart, it left him feeling exposed.

The older woman hardly seemed fazed by his question, but sighed heavily and shook her head and pulled out two large chunks of dark dried meat with crinkling white bakery tissue and handed one to each of them. Slade's stomach grumbled. While meat wouldn't do much to stem his hunger, it couldn't hurt, so he took a bite. The combination of salt and sweet, heated with pepper, filled his mouth. The taste and texture sparked another profound feeling of déjà vu.

"She was one of us. Long time ago. So sad. You should take a lesson from that one." She shook an admonishing finger at Raina. "That girl was chosen like you. Never would stay home. Had to go see the big world. And the big world swallowed her up." The older woman's fingers snapped together like a biting mouth.

"I haven't gone anywhere," Raina mumbled around a mouthful of jerky.

Auntie Mo clucked. "City's no place for the likes of us, Whisperer, mark my words."

Raina turned away from her aunt and Slade noted that she rolled her eyes as she did so, but that she didn't argue with the woman. Officer nature girl started gathering up an armful of foodstuffs from the aisles and snatched up a couple of gallons of water for their trek.

What Slade didn't realize was his momentary drift in attention had left him open for attack. "As for you…" Auntie Mo shook a plump, well-creased finger at him. "You Blackwolfs have had your share of sadness. Dark things happen to you. Make amends with the ancestors and things should go better."

Slade quirked a brow at the woman. "How can you be so sure you know who I am?" He was confident she'd never seen a vampire before.

Her mouth split into a knowing smile. "We know our own, little Blackwolf."

An image of Auntie Mo, her hair black, threaded with the start of silver at the temples, filled his mind. Her utter certainty bit down hard on him, painful and sharp. Other than the vampire clan, he hadn't known any kind of family, at least none that he could remember. So why the hell did he clearly remember this woman, only much younger?

"I'm sorry, have we ever met before?"

The old woman chuckled. "Don't remember me, eh? No matter. Probably better you don't. Dark times they were. Dark times."

Slade was even more puzzled.

He helped Raina unload her armful of goods onto the counter and watched Auntie Mo's arthritic fingers make short work of efficiently packing the sacks, then stared out the window at the gravel lot and the distant pines, feeling antsy as hell and wanting to be gone.

"Ready?" Raina's voice startled him.

He gave her no other answer than a quick, firm nod as she tossed three twenty-dollar bills down on the counter, picked up two grocery bags, then jerked her chin to indicate he pick up the other two.

"You children be careful out in the woods," Auntie Mo called out over the chime of the bell on the door.

Raina gave a halfhearted wave and made a beeline to her car, tossing the bags into the backseat. He followed her example. Hell, as far as he was concerned, the sooner he got done with this little adventure to natureville, the better.

Slade picked up a curious mixture of embarrassment and annoyance scenting the air with bubblegum and smoke as Raina started the car and pulled back out onto the main road through town. Clearly, while she knew and liked the older woman, there were things left unspoken between them that nature girl didn't want to deal with.

There were a number of things Auntie Mo had said that had piqued Slade's curiosity. Why was she so thoroughly convinced that she knew who his mother was? Why had she called Officer Ravenwing *Whisperer?* And what in the hell had the old woman meant by being *chosen?* Slade chewed on the ideas along with his piece of beef jerky as they turned off the narrow paved road up a gravel track. He was better off not knowing, he told himself. He needed focus. The more focus he had the sooner he could go back to pounding a beer or two with the other members of the security team and playing poker during the day.

* * *

Raina gave up trying to tune anything in on the radio. They were far enough away from the towers, and hemmed in by mountains so big the signals didn't make it through. Only the static on her police scanner made any noise at all.

The relative silence that had stretched between them was broken by the deep, dark timbre of Donovan's voice. "So why do they call it Jake's if it's run by your aunt?"

"Jake was Mo's husband. And she's not really my aunt. Not by blood, anyway. Well, not direct blood relation." She was botching her explanation, but the relationship was complicated. "She's more like a great-aunt several times removed. As a sign of affection and respect, our tribe calls all older male and female relations on the mother's side *secs*—which translates into aunt and uncle."

He fixed those disconcerting topaz-colored eyes on her and for a moment Raina held her breath. It was as though he could see straight through her and into her head, peeling apart her memories, her dreams and her fears like the segments of an orange. He turned his gaze back out toward the looming mountains and she exhaled a sigh of relief.

"Why'd she call you Whisperer? That your middle name?"

"Are you just trying to make conversation? Because it's not really necessary, Mr. Donovan."

"Slade. If we're going to be working on this together

for more than twenty-four hours you might as well call me Slade."

"Fine. Slade. Whatever."

"So?"

"So what?"

"Why'd she call you Whisperer?"

Raina tightened her grip on the steering wheel. "I don't think that's really any of your business."

"For the sake of argument let's say it would help me to understand what we're looking at with these wolves."

"I don't see how it could."

"Why?"

"Because it's all a bunch of tribal myth and legend. Folklore. Nothing that could possibly help us in this very real situation we've got with these flesh-and-blood wolves."

"Humor me."

Raina heaved a heavy sigh. "It's my calling."

"To not talk loudly?"

She threw him a withering glare. "The full name is Wolf Whisperer."

"Which has nothing to do with wolves, because…"

"Because the wolves I'm supposed to be able to whisper to are actually the embodiment of our ancestors' spirits, okay? That enough hocus-pocus for you?"

Slade chuckled.

"What, now you're going to make fun of me for it?"

He put up his hands in mock surrender. "Me. No."

"Then why are you laughing?"

"Because you get so worked up about it. It's just a name, babe. Not your whole world."

Raina let the slight pass and gave a mirthless little laugh. "I wish it were that easy." She paused, choosing her next words carefully because they ached in her chest. "In my tribe, the name is everything. There is only one chosen Wolf Whisperer in a generation. One who is selected by the elders to be the tribe's connection to the ancestors' knowledge, protection, healing and justice." The last word made her want to gag.

She'd seen the justice meted out by the ancestors when she was little. It had been horrifying. Kaycee Blackwolf had been ripped to pieces by the superhuman-size wolves while the tribal members had turned their backs and walked away. Just another reason she didn't really want to be the Whisperer at all.

The fact that Kaycee had been Slade's mother wasn't lost on her. If anything, it made it all worse. Truly he was the last person she should be getting help from— he was *qelaen*—an outcast who caused others to turn away, because of his mother's actions. But telling him the intricacies of tribal lore and law weren't going to score her any points with him right now, so she was better off to keep it to herself.

Blackwolf had been the Whisperer of her generation and Raina was in no mood to follow in her shoes. Rather than run from the tribe like Kaycee had, Raina had done everything she could to embrace the role in a different way by helping bring the tribe into the twenty-first century. She'd gone to college, learned natural resource science, gone to the police academy and gotten a job as a game warden with the state to protect the animals they valued and their rights to hunt the land, as well as bring modern justice to the tribe.

Since the night of Blackwolf's tribunal and execution, the oversize wolves had not been seen or heard from. That was until a month ago, when rumors starting flying. Three attacks, two on livestock and one on a human, had put Raina smack-dab in the middle of a clash between local authorities, tribal interest and the wolves.

She'd chalked it up to developers nosing around the river valley and farther up into the hills aggravating the wildlife, but now she wasn't so sure.

"What about Auntie Mo's mix-up?"

His question snapped her out of her thoughts. "Mix-up?"

"Yeah. I assume the reason you came to the clan calling me Blackwolf is because she was mixed up."

"There is no mix-up. Auntie Mo was right, Kaycee Donovan Blackwolf *was* your mother."

Slade snorted. "Lady, I don't have any memories of my mother or my father. So you're talking to a wall."

"Tell you what. When we're done interviewing Joseph, we'll hop down to Ellensburg and you can look up the county records for yourself."

Of course she already knew what was there. She'd investigated it herself to find him in the first place. While Kaycee was Slade's mother, no father had been listed on the birth certificate, which kind of made Raina wonder if that was the reason the tribunal had let the wolves take her.

"Sounds like you've already done that."

Raina slid him a cautious sideways glance beneath her lashes. Slade Donovan Blackwolf was not a man to be toyed with. All the way from Seattle to Teanachee she'd wondered if she might expire from lack of oxygen in the car. He seemed to soak up the air around him. There was no point in playing games with him. He'd need to know the truth sooner or later.

"I have."

He grunted. "Since you seem to have all the answers, if this Kaycee Blackwolf was my mother, who was my father?"

Raina gave a little shrug. "I'm sorry. There was no father's name listed." Raina couldn't imagine what it would be like not knowing who her parents were. Her mom and dad had made her who she was. He could only have been eight or nine years old when Kaycee had been murdered. Where had he gone? Who'd raised him? Curiosity ate at her, but she schooled her features not to give away the questions tumbling around in her head.

He was here for one thing, and one thing only. She needed his unique set of skills to track down the elusive large wolves. And once she'd accomplished that, she had to get as far away from him as possible before she, too, became another sad tribal tale.

His dark brows beetled together until they nearly met in the middle over the bridge of his strong, straight nose. If Donovan didn't like hearing that, he certainly wasn't going to like hearing how his mother had died.

"So what happened? She decide a kid was an inconvenience, and dumped me off somewhere to be raised by vampires?"

Raina felt an answering ache of sympathy in her chest and chose her words with care. "Your mother had an accident."

She tightened her grip on the steering wheel even more as she felt Slade turn those whiskey eyes on her. His searing gaze heated her skin uncomfortably.

"What kind of accident?"

Raina hesitated, unsure if now was really the time to be discussing this subject. "She was killed by wolves."

All the color drained from Slade's already pale skin. "Did you say wolves?"

Raina swallowed hard and nodded.

"How long until we get in range of cell service?"

"Why?"

"I got a call to make."

Chapter 4

Slade pocketed his useless phone in disgust. Joseph Edgewater's spread was way the hell too desolate for cell service. It had taken another tense and awkwardly silent half hour to show up at the small single-story farmhouse with a wide, sagging, covered front porch and collection of outbuildings that looked like they'd been around since the turn of the century. The roof on the barn had been patched so many times it resembled a crazy quilt.

He could try to talk to Achilles with his mind, but about now he imagined his commander was sleeping deeply beside his wife and wouldn't appreciate the wake-up call by conventional or unconventional means. The questions zipping around in Slade's brain had waited this long, and could wait a few hours more. In particular the ones about how he'd come to the clan and if they'd known his mother. But regardless, he couldn't shake off the feeling that there was something Raina was still hiding from him.

"How long do you think this'll take?" he asked as he pried himself out of her little car.

Raina got out, closed the vehicle's door and looked around, her eyes narrowing, then shifted her gaze to him. "Depends on how good a tracker you are."

Slade gave her a confident smirk. "Why didn't you say so? Hell, we might make it back to Seattle for a late dinner." It sounded cocky, he knew, but then he had a right to be. While his kind were known for having highly developed senses, his abilities were off the charts even for a vampire.

He started to scan the trees, sniffing the air and looking for anything to give a hint that the Weres had been present.

The screen over the front door slapped shut and a man in his mid-fifties, dressed in worn denim overalls, a red plaid shirt and tan hunting boots, came lumbering down the steps of the wide covered porch toward them. Raina waved in greeting. "Afternoon Joe!"

He nodded, halfheartedly returning Raina's wave. A ratty blue baseball cap shaded the man's face, but even through the shadows Slade could see the wariness in his dark eyes. Slade wondered if it was his presence or that of a police officer.

"Who's your friend?" Joseph asked as his attention swiveled back to fix on Raina. Clearly, Joe was just fine with the police officer.

"A wolf expert." She made introductions, and Slade shook the man's hand. Joe smelled of strong coffee, bacon and a hint of fishing bait. But underneath those stronger smells, the scent of fear, metallic and coppery like a new penny, clung to the older man, as well as the musty scent of sorrow. Slade would bet he'd lost some-one recently and by deduction guessed it was to the wolves. Why else would she bring him way out here first?

"Have those wolves been back to bother you again?" Raina's tone echoed her concern.

Joe, obviously a man of very few words, just shook his head in reply and stared past Slade's shoulder to the tree line. Slade turned and tried to pinpoint the place that fixated his interest. A shadow of movement at the edge of the trees caught his attention. He telescoped his vision, able to pick out individual pine needles and ridges in the fat hanging pinecones from five hundred yards away. There in the dirt among the detritus of dried needles and grasses was the impression of a paw print.

A print far bigger than a normal timber wolf or cougar, and closer to the size of a bear—or a Were.

Slade inhaled deeply, catching a faint whiff of wet canine mixed with pine pitch and the metallic bite of blood—dried but there nonetheless. Joseph Edgewater was a sitting duck this close to Were territory. His fear said he knew it.

Raina's touch on his arm jerked Slade's attention back to her. "Did you see something?"

"Just my imagination," he replied smoothly. There

was more going on here than Joe was saying. The place reeked of Were. As much as Slade hated to do it with Raina right there beside him, he spoke slowly and deliberately to Joe, sending out a glamour to muddle the man's mind so he could infiltrate his thoughts. "Tell me what you know about the wolves, Joe."

Joe's pupils dilated slightly, growing round as the glamour took effect. "They took Robbie. Police say it was animal attack, but Robbie's not dead. I know he's not dead."

Slade sifted through the images in Joe's mind. His teenage boy's face. A frantic search over the property. The open door of an old pickup truck abandoned and still running. "But you think he's lost or been taken."

Joe nodded, his eyes growing shiny with unshed tears.

More images pelted Slade now. A trail of blood on the ground. A single hunting boot, half torn apart, lost among the brush. "And you're afraid he's not coming back."

Joe pulled on the rim of his hat then sniffed hard, wiping the back of his hand across his nose. "He won't come back. They made sure of that."

"The wolves?"

Raina inserted herself between them. Instantly, Joe's eyes cleared and the wariness was back. His lips paled as they pressed firmly together and the glamour faded. Slade decided right then and there that Officer Ravenwing was not only interfering but also an annoyance he'd be better off without.

"Look, I've already talked to him about all of this,"

she said firmly. "Can't you see it distresses him? All we need to do is find out if there's anything left to track."

"Don't know what the point of you being here is," Joe muttered. "Like I already told Raina, no matter what we do now, he ain't coming back."

"Has this happened to anyone else?" Slade asked, determined to get some kind of straight answer.

"Nobody's said as much."

Slade speared Raina with a questioning glance: why were they even here?

"You mind if we look around a bit?" she asked, her voice upbeat and professional.

"Go right on ahead, Whisperer. If anyone could talk to Robbie, it'd be you."

Slade nodded at Joe then set off for the tree line. Raina turned quickly, right on his heels. There'd been something slinking around the spot recently. In fact, he'd bet it was still somewhere on that mountain. As fast as Weres could be, they couldn't transport like a vampire. To move, they had to run, and if they ran, they left prints and scents that could be tracked.

Slade reached out to his commander, knowing he'd be concerned about the extent Weres had already infiltrated the mortal community.

This had better be important, Achilles answered his voice curt.

They're taking people in the community.

Are you sure it wasn't voluntary?

Hard to tell until I talk to one. I'd have to track down the boy. And Achilles—we need to talk. I know you've been holding back about my past.

The silence was deafening and set Slade on edge. *Achilles?*

We'll talk when you get back. For now, see what you can find out about the pack's activities. If they're on the move, I want to know why.

Slade glanced at Raina as she trotted along beside him. The sound of her slightly uneven breathing, and the elevated pace of her heart as she tried to catch up with him, was very similar to how she'd sound during lovemaking. Slade ruthlessly pushed the thought away, but couldn't get the image out of his mind of her breasts moving beneath her shirt as she jogged.

"Anyone ever tell you that you're a little too focused?" she said with slight asperity. "I'm guessing you've already got a place in mind you'd like to start."

He slowed his pace slightly to adjust to hers, realizing while he was slow for a vampire he was moving too fast for a mortal. "There was something in the trees that caught Joe's attention." He didn't go into detail. There was no reason to pull her deeper into this potentially lethal situation.

The light changed as they reached the big trees and were cast into shifting shadows. Late-summer heat brought out the fragrant resin of the trees and heated the oils in the needles, making the forest smell like a cross between a Christmas tree lot and newly cut lumber. A perfect blind for whoever, whatever, was moving ahead of them. Their scent was harder to track with such strong smells overpowering them.

Crouching, Slade touched the hand-span indentation in the earth of a paw print. "You say the big wolves haven't been around in a long time. Just how long?"

Dappled sunlight filtering through the branches high overhead highlighted her ebony hair, making her dark brown eyes glow with vitality. She was a pretty woman, with fine skin and an athletic feminine frame, but that uniform did little for her. "About twenty-five years."

Just about twenty-five years ago he'd woken up in a Dumpster in Seattle, without a clue who he was or how he'd gotten there, his foot bleeding and injured. He'd lived on the streets long enough to develop a healthy aversion to cops. "Last time they were here, were there other disappearances similar to Robbie's?"

"I don't know." She tucked the sweep of her hair behind her ear. "We could ask Auntie Mo. She'd remember."

He'd save that as a last resort. Slade stared up through the maze of tree trunks. There wasn't nearly the amount of understory on this side of the mountains as there was in the woods on the western face of the Cascades, allowing him to see much farther.

About two hundred yards up the mountain a brief flash of brown fur caught his attention. It moved too close to the ground to be a deer or elk and it was too big for a coyote. The wind changed direction and the smell of wolf filled his nose. Just how close to the pack's main den were they?

"You'd better go grab your supplies. We're going in on foot from here on out." For the moment he was profoundly glad nature girl knew how to put her boots on and rough it. It would have made his job so much harder to have a girl in strappy little heels who needed bottled water just to walk a flight of stairs.

He kept an eye on Raina as she jogged back to her car and pulled out her trusty hiking pack, stuffing some of the food and a gallon of the water into it before she slung it onto her back. By the time she made it to the tree line, Slade was down on one knee examining the earth closely. The thought of helping her with her gear flitted across his mind. But then, given their uneasy partnership, she'd probably take it as a sign he thought she couldn't do her job. He'd wait until she really needed his help.

"Found a trail?"

He pointed to the large paw print outline. "Whatever made this was here recently." He looked at her. "When did Robbie disappear?"

"Two weeks ago."

Slade's jaw flexed and tightened. He touched the center of the print with his fingertips, then sniffed them. Dirt heavy with iron, a fast-flowing stream and saxifrage plant that only grew in high alpine conditions. "The thing that made this print was here in the last two hours."

A shiver shimmed down Raina's spine, making her skin pebble. He could almost hear the small downy hairs lifting on her arms.

As much as she wanted to protect her friends and discover more about the wolves, she was still ultimately unsettled by them. Score one for his side. Wary was better than foolish.

"So are we just going to scout up the hill until

dusk?" she asked as she readjusted the loaded pack on her back.

"No, I was planning on heading out. Wasn't it you who said we'd be wasting time if we didn't get here sooner than later?"

"But it's only a few hours until dark."

"You afraid of the dark?"

"Hardly, but if we're going overnight camping, then we're going to need a tent and sleeping bags."

"You have them in your car?"

She nodded.

"Go ahead and grab them."

"What about you? I know you didn't bring that kind of gear and I've only got one sleeping bag."

Slade gave her a bone-melting smile and materialized at his feet his military pack from the car. "Don't need a sleeping bag or a tent, babe. Vampire, remember?"

Raina resisted the urge to roll her eyes. "So what's in there?" She pointed at his black bag.

"Weapons. Explosives. Toothpaste. The usual."

"Wait!" She made a grab for his bag, but he swung it away from her reach. "Explosives? What on earth makes you think we'll need that kind of hardware?"

"Luck favors the prepared. You should know that better than most. Wolves aren't the only ones out on state land. Ever met a pissed-off bear? Not anything you want to tangle with hand-to-hand."

Raina harrumphed. "Bears," she muttered as she turned on her heel and marched back to her car. "Poachers are more dangerous than bears. I'm going to get my overnight camping gear and see if Joe minds me parking for a night or two."

Fifteen minutes later she was ready to go again and the shadows of the trees were beginning to stretch and grow longer as the day began to wane.

The overnight hiking pack weighed close to fifty pounds and was half as large as she was, extended up above her head. A bedroll and lightweight tent, as well as some freeze-dried supplies, a water purifier, a first-aid kit, a few utensils and extra ammunition. He contemplated asking her if she'd like him to carry it. Given the stubborn tilt of her chin, he'd bet she'd take it as an insult.

Slade eyed the pack. "You sure you didn't bring the kitchen sink?"

"Why, did you think we might need one?" she threw back at him, matching his sarcastic tone. "At least I didn't pack explosives."

Slade chuckled. "You've got spunk, Officer, I'll give you that. What about jelly beans. Got any of those?"

"How would they help?"

"Sweet tooth."

Raina rolled her eyes, checked the heavily padded shoulder straps and made sure everything was adjusted correctly, then smiled. "Let's go find the big, bad wolf."

Chapter 5

She could make light of it all she wanted to, but Slade knew the reality. Every step they took into the wilderness sent them deeper into Were territory, which meant he needed to be on full alert to every smell, scent and sound.

He just couldn't tell *her* that. Mortals had been skittish enough discovering vampires lived among them, and the Council had decided information about other supernaturals, like the Weres, was to be kept strictly on a need-to-know basis. And they didn't need to know.

Not yet, anyway.

They climbed farther through the trees continuing up the slope of the mountain. The early evening sunlight spilled through breaks in the evergreen boughs like spears of gold casting their path into a tangled mix of light and dark. Night would be on them in a matter of hours. The days were getting shorter as summer slipped into fall. He inhaled and caught the scent of frost, sharp and clean, coming on the night air mixed with the fading wet-dog scent of Were and the salty sweetness of the perspiration on Raina's skin.

Slade relied far more on scent than sight or hearing when he tracked. Hearing anything was a challenge when Raina's rapid, rhythmic breathing and the blood rushing in her veins sounded like a fast-flowing river to him. Tracking tonight was more difficult than usual with the increasing tightness starting in his muscles. The first sign of moon sickness. He was focused on sorting through the array of sensory input he picked up, when her voice distracted him, putting him on edge.

"As long as we're headed up the ridge, we might want to drop by and see Auntie Lee." She was only slightly breathless, and certainly holding her own. But how long would that last?

That made Slade hesitate a step as he turned and gave her a wry glance. "Auntie Lee?" He wasn't absolutely positive he wanted to know the answer.

"She's a retired midwife. Her cabin is about a four-hour hike in this direction."

He bet it lay smack in the middle of Were territory. "How about you do that another time." His voice was a little gruff, even to his own ears, but he was gritting his teeth against the firelike heat beginning to spread through his limbs. The sun hadn't even fully set yet, and already the moon's pull was strong.

"Fine. I just thought you might like to talk to her. I

wasn't going to suggest it before, but since it looked like we were headed by her place regardless, and seeing as how she delivered you—"

He whipped around and grabbed her upper arm hard enough to cause her to jerk to a stop. "She what?"

"She delivered you. She was the local midwife when you were born."

Slade shook his head. "How do you know this stuff?"

"She's Auntie Mo's sister. In a town this size it's not hard to find someone who knows something about everything."

Strike two against small towns, Slade thought.

She paused just long enough that Slade knew she was holding something vital back. "And?" he demanded.

"And she was named on your birth certificate."

Ding. Ding. We have a winner. And a little good news for once. Maybe this aunt knew something about what caused his moon sickness. About who his father had been and why he'd been dumped in this place. More importantly, if she'd been around that long, maybe she knew what the hell was going on with the Weres and how to stop it so they could all get back to their normal lives.

An hour later they reached the rocky crag atop the mountain only to find it was a foothill to a larger ridge. Down below the forest spread out in a dark, fragrant carpet of evergreen. The dying rays of the sun threw the gathering clouds in a pastel-rippled rainbow of orange, reds, pinks and purples as it set in between the jagged peaks of the Alpine Lakes Wilderness Area.

He was deliberately moving slow, letting her set the pace, but the delay in getting to wherever this Were trail led was killing him. Normally he enjoyed the fall of night, but not tonight, not with the waxing moon five days away from being full. He glanced back at Raina to make sure she was still keeping up.

Raina shifted her weight from one foot to the next. The pack was digging uncomfortably into her shoulders and her lower back was already beginning to ache. It had been a long time since she'd packed a full camp more than four hours into the wilderness. "We really should make camp for the night before it gets full dark."

The vampire threw her an incredulous look. "When night is just coming on? Hell, I'm just starting to wake up, babe."

"Fine, then why don't you keep going and come back and get me in the morning? It isn't safe to hike at night. There are a hundred dangers, not the least of which would be falling down a ravine."

"That's only if you have human vision. The dark actually makes it easier for me to see, at least until the moon rises."

"Then you turn into a pumpkin?"

"Wrong fairy tale."

"Please tell me you're not going to turn into a bat."

The corner of his lip twitched with humor. "Nothing so dramatic. The moonlight is just too bright when it's nearly full and it can give me a migraine same as daylight if I'm out in it too long."

Raina did some quick calculations in her head. "So maybe another three hours until moonrise. Can we compromise on that and make camp then?"

Slade nodded.

"Shake on it."

He grasped her hand fully in his much larger one. The contact set off that familiar arc of awareness that had sparkled straight up her arm when she'd touched him at the clan compound, making her whole body tighten with desire and need. Raina gasped at the sensation, knowing her eyes had grown wider. The touch seemed to impact him just as much as it had her. His nostrils flared and his mouth slightly parted, like he wanted to eat her.

"Do you want me to carry that pack for you?"

"No. I'm fine." Raina quickly pulled her hand from his grasp. She thought the spark between them had been a fluke. Apparently not. Even more reason for her to avoid her natural attraction to the bad-boy vibe he was throwing off. "If you want to make it to Auntie Lee's, we'd better get going."

He snapped his mouth shut without another word and whipped her around, yanking the pack off her back and hefting it over his own shoulders. "No point in you carrying this load the whole time." The weight being lifted from her shoulders and spine made her feel instantly like she was floating and almost weightless.

She tried to thank him, but before her lips could even form the words he stalked up the darkening trail, leaving her to catch up. Raina tried to stick close to the vampire, knowing he could see what she couldn't in the woods. There was no need for a flashlight. Her eyes adjusted to the growing dimness, but even now the sky was lighter than normal with the first rays of a rising moon.

The shifting shadows brought darker thoughts to mind. What if the legends of her people weren't just tall tales? She knew plenty about pack dynamics of regular wolves, but what if there was a deeper connection between her tribe and these wolves than she'd ever imagined? Just thinking that somehow this might all rest on her shoulders made her feel as if her hiking pack was once again on her back, weighing down the movement of her feet.

"Are you wearing out on me, Officer?" Slade called out over his shoulder. She suspected he could be miles ahead of her, but he was moderating his pace to accommodate her.

Lord, the man could move fast. And he was strong. He had her hiking pack slung on one shoulder and his black bag in his hand as if each were no more than a plastic grocery sack filled with a bag of potato chips.

Even though she no longer carried the pack, her muscles screamed. Suddenly Slade froze in the path, the line of his back rigid. He put the pack and duffel down soundlessly beside him on the path and, without looking back, motioned with his hand for her to crouch low.

Sensing something was off, she didn't question him, and instantly sank to her haunches, curving her back to make herself as small as possible. For several minutes she thought that perhaps he was overreacting. Other than the faint rustle of leaves overhead, she couldn't hear anything other than her own breathing, and the unsteady thump of her heartbeat.

Then she heard it—faintly at first. The husky yips and panting of a pair of wolves up ahead riveted her attention. She and Slade were almost to Auntie Lee's cabin.

With amazing stealth, Slade inched his way back to her, placing his index finger to his lips, telling her to remain quiet. Since she still couldn't see what he saw, she focused instead on his mouth. He had firm lips, but they were sensual, made for long, slow kisses by a warm, crackling fire on a blanket-strewn floor. Now whose imagination was running away with them? Raina berated herself. How foolish to indulge in such fantasies when she barely knew him. The snuffling of the creatures faded and only the night sounds of crickets, scuttling mice and an occasional hoot from an owl mixed with the shushing wind in the trees.

"Was it them?" she whispered.

He just glanced at her, the line of his jaw growing rigid, making the dent in his chin seem even deeper. "Just stick close to me and stay quiet." He moved back to the discarded packs and slung them back over his shoulder, motioning her to follow him with a crook of his finger.

Raina sighed and sauntered up to him.

Stick close. The words were simple enough, but certainly brought to mind a whole host of more carnal thoughts. Slade was a good-looking—oh, who the hell was she kidding?—he was a phenomenally good-looking man. The kind that was just rough enough around the edges, and smoldering hot to make women weak in the knees and wet in the panties. Sticking close to him wasn't exactly a hardship—unless you didn't want to be involved with a bad boy on any level. Which described her to a T—for temptation.

The last bad boy she'd tangled with had almost convinced her to walk away from her tribe and never look back. Screw their old legends, Rocky had said. They're just a bunch of hokey stories. And Lord how she wanted to believe him. It would have made being chosen the Whisperer after Kaycee's death so much easier to bear if it meant nothing—if she hadn't had the terrifying scene branded into her memory as a child.

But Raina knew to the tribe it meant everything.

In times of trouble the Wolf Whisperer was the link—the connection—between the worlds of the spirit ancestors and the tribe. Break the link by eliminating a Whisperer who had yet to bear a child, and the link would disappear forever. Her people's connection to their ancestors would be broken. So she'd left Rocky one night when he'd passed out after a wild party, gotten herself enrolled at the police academy, and never looked back.

Until now.

There was no way someone like Slade would give up his world to become part of hers, was he going to go from bad-boy vampire to respectable normal citizen. Who was she kidding? Good grief, they weren't even in the same species, if the rumors and news reports going around the scientific community about DNA mutated by viruses were correct.

She was *Homo sapiens*.

He was *Homo lamia*.

A different breed altogether. Like gray wolves and red wolves, the same but totally different. They could coexist, but they sure as hell shouldn't mix.

"Are we close to the wolf territory?" Small bubbles of excitement fizzed in her veins. She'd been over this stretch of mountains before, when Robbie had first gone missing, but hadn't found anything.

"Yeah." He hesitated, not sounding excited in the least. "Listen, this sounded like a good plan earlier, but I think it'd be a better idea for you to make camp and in the morning head back down the mountain."

Raina's first reaction was to pull her revolver out on him and ask why, but she refrained. "But we're almost to my aunt's place."

"Yeah," he said as he sniffed the air, "and we're getting damn close to that pack's den."

Wasn't that just like a guy to do a U-turn right when you thought he could handle the driving? "Don't be ridiculous. I didn't climb halfway up a mountainside to turn tail and scurry back to town. I'm a trained professional. I think I can handle it."

"Trust me, they didn't train you for this."

His distinct lack of confidence in her abilities had gone from annoying to pissing her off. "Look, Donovan, I'm not going anywhere. I came to observe them, see if there's really a valid reason for concern. It's unusual for wolves to be up here in the first place. If they've migrated over from the packs in Idaho or Montana, it's important that I know. And besides, people are frightened of *something*. It's my job to discover what that is. That hasn't changed." She turned on her booted heel and took two steps away from him before he grabbed her.

He held her by the shoulders and forced her to look him in the eye. "They've got good reason to be scared. Trust me."

There was no way she could move without brushing up against the rock-hard body she'd been staring at all evening as they had climbed deeper into the trees.

He wasn't much of a conversationalist, which left her mind plenty of time to indulge in her healthy imagination. Like what exactly Slade Donovan's ass looked like underneath those jeans. The color of his eyes almost looked like molten gold in the flash of the moon's growing light.

"Look, there's got to be a reason these wolves are approaching humans. It's atypical behavior for wolves to do so—they're territorial creatures who tend to stick to their packs and stay away from humans. Maybe Robbie and his friends were hunting them down. Maybe developers are pushing too far in on their territory."

He closed his eyes tight, little lines of frustration creasing his temples. "No, you don't get it."

"Then why don't you enlighten me, Mr. Expert."

His eyes opened slowly, and the tawny recesses of them seemed to draw her in, mesmerizing in their intensity. "These wolves aren't normal."

Well, duh! "Why do you think I called you out here?"

She pulled away from his hold, brushing up against him, the contact making her skin contract. "I know they're a unique species. They're huge, super strong—"

This time he pushed her up against a tree, the move surprising and swift. The rough bark dug sharply into his knuckles as he kept her backed against the tree. He shouldn't have touched her, Slade knew.

The scent of her skin made his hands itch to touch her, while the rapid beat of her heart and the susurrus of her blood beneath her skin, a living tide of heat and life, made his fangs ache. But he tamped down the need threatening to overtake his senses. He waited until she looked fully into his eyes. "Stop going off half-cocked and listen up."

She gave a heavy sigh.

Damn it. Was she ready for this? Would she understand what he was about to tell her, and if so, how would she react? She'd had a belief system her entire life, and he was about to blow that all to hell. Her eyes narrowed as she looked up at him, annoyance stiffening every line of her body. She was a woman who liked to do things her way. Well, that was all well and good until faced with what she was about to face.

"These wolves aren't *wolves*."

Worry flickered behind her confident stare. "Of course they're *Canis lupus*. I've seen them. Yeah, they're big, but what else could they possibly be?"

"They're shape-shifters…Weres."

The moonlight painted her feminine profile in a soft

pearlescent glow, making her seem almost pale enough to be vampire.

"Wait a second. Weres? As in werewolves, is that what you're trying to tell me?" Her whole body relaxed and shook beneath his hands as she smothered her laughter. "Werewolves?"

Slade wasn't laughing. He didn't even crack a smirk. The cramping pain in his muscles was turning to a smoldering fire under his skin. "Until a year ago people didn't believe vampires were real, either."

All Raina's joviality immediately evaporated. She gasped, her eyes narrowing, shadows shifting over her face as she pulled against his hold on her. "You're serious, aren't you? You really think these wolves are half human? And I thought my tribe had some wild tall tales about the ancestors."

"No. As I said the first time, I think they're shape-shifters."

She frowned. "So how can you say they took Robbie?"

"They didn't take him. They converted him."

"Into a shape-shifter?"

Slade quirked a brow at her. "Well, they didn't transform him into a Pomeranian."

"B-but, how?"

"Same way vampires transform humans into our own kind, by introducing a colonizing virus into their bodies that their immune system can't override. But it's a different virus—much more virulent than the vampire variety. The virus that creates vampires takes a much higher quantity and the body has to be almost depleted of its ability to fight it off. The Were virus activates with a single bite. Once the saliva penetrates the skin, that's all she wrote. Transformation can take place by the next full moon."

The stunned look on Raina's face was priceless. He doubted he'd ever see her-know-it-all-ness quiet again. "But they have all the characteristics and habits of wolves. There's nothing supernatural about them beyond their size."

Slade shrugged. It wasn't a question, but he answered it anyway. "How could you even tell? In either their wolf or their human form, they have a very defined hierarchy that follows pack law."

A light of understanding brightened her eyes. "You vampires don't like shape-shifters, do you?"

Slade gritted his teeth and deliberately ignored her question as he let go of her. "How far did you say it was to your aunt's cabin?"

She raised a dark brow, calling his bluff. "Answer the question, Donovan."

"No. We don't normally interact with Weres. They stay on their side of the mountains and we stay on ours."

She bit her bottom lip, making him far too aware of what it might feel like to kiss her.

"That explains why you are jumpy about cruising over their territory."

"You don't know the half of it, babe," he replied. Slade fisted his hands, then relaxed them, trying to control the growing pain centered in his gut He'd been through the drill enough to know that his moon sickness was worse than normal. If he could get her to the safety of her aunt's cabin, then perhaps he could transport back to the clan's medical center for treatment for an hour or two, then transport back before she woke.

Raina took out her backlit GPS and glanced at the reading. "It should be an hour that way. Just at the base of Red Top Mountain." She pointed up toward the rocks that pushed definitely upward out of the trees dead on in the direction of the Were pack's den.

"I thought you said we were almost there."

She glanced back at him. "Out here, that's just around the block."

From the smell of things, in one hour they could be at the pack's front door. She had no idea just what dangers lay up ahead.

Slade did, and even for him, the hair on the back of his neck was lifted. He opened his senses wide and tested the air. But the winds had shifted. Instead of Were he smelled aroused female flesh and sweet blood.

His fangs throbbed so hard the ache made his face feel like it was splitting in two.

"We'd better get moving." Halfway up the ridge the moon came out in all her pale glory. The cramps moved from his stomach, pulsating out into his arms and legs, making him shake uncontrollably from the pain.

Silently, Slade screamed, *No! No! Damn it, no!* The moon sickness was taking him over and he'd be unable to protect Raina. She couldn't sense the Weres like he could. She'd never even know they were coming until it was too late.

He staggered and bit the inside of his mouth, releasing a flood of ichor across his tongue as the pain grew. Son of a bitch. He fell against a tree trunk with his shoulder. If he'd been mortal, he would have passed out long ago or been panting hard. But with no need to breathe, all he could do was focus on putting one foot in front of the other, ignoring the burning pulse of pain, until he got her to the cabin.

An hour away? He doubted he'd be conscious in the next ten minutes.

"Since you've been to your aunt's before, why don't you lead the way from here," he suggested.

Raina came up from behind him on the trail and nodded, then took the lead. It was really too bad he couldn't enjoy the view more. Even through the painfully plain olive-green uniform pants the flair of her hips and the curve of her ass made an enticing display as they swayed from side to side while she walked.

Slade stumbled again and fell to one knee. His fangs, brought out by the pain, descended from his soft gum tissue, just above his teeth, with an audible *flick.* Raina moved farther away, the dark all but consuming her. He had to get up. He had to make sure she survived. The Weres were too close, and if they caught her they'd either kill her or transform her.

Small explosions popped and seared through his skeletal system, every joint feeling like it had been shot at close range by a revolver.

He collapsed to the forest floor with a groan, his face buried in the prickly needles. Slade convulsed, clutched at the raw hot pain tearing through him as the edges of his vision darkened.

"Slade!" Raina raced back, her footsteps sliding in the leaves, and fell to her knees beside him, turning him over on his back and staring deep into his eyes, her brow creased with worry. "Are you hurt? What's wrong?"

He tried to speak, but couldn't. The moon sickness had been bad before, but never this bad. Perhaps he'd gone too long without feeding. Perhaps it had just progressed beyond the point he could manage it anymore. The vamp doctors had said all along it might reach a point where he should be confined to the clan's medical facilities when it came on. He gritted his teeth hard, his fangs piercing his bottom lip.

"Slade! Answer me!"

The best he could do was groan as fire erupted beneath his skin, burning away reason and rational thought. He fought the pain, fought whatever was happening in his body down to the very last cell until he blacked out.

He woke to find himself in the confines of a small tent shaped like a turtle shell. It was meant for two, but barely stretched shoulder to shoulder for him. The translucent fabric tinted the streaming pale morning light royal blue. He stretched, testing his boundaries, and encountered a soft warm female curled up along his left side.

Sometime between when he'd passed out and when he'd woken she had removed her uniform and bra, changing into a T-shirt and jeans. That left only the thin fabric of her shirt between his chest and the soft globes of her breasts. And when he should have pulled away, that fact alone drove him to pull her closer.

She stirred but didn't wake, brushing her mouth against his bare chest. The whisper of her lips along his fevered skin was a cool, soft caress. She rolled over, exposing her neck and the delicate shell of her ear. The dark fall of her sleep-mussed hair slid over his sensitized skin like a ripple of silk, making the heat escalate inside him for an entirely different reason.

Slade inhaled, not because he needed to fill his useless lungs, but because he wanted to indulge in the unusual spicy-sweet strawberry-and-gunpowder scent of her. He ached to have a taste of her just to see if her skin tasted as delicious as it smelled, and hot damn was he hungry. He always was after tangling with his odd condition.

He curled around her, wrapping his arm about her waist and bringing the curve of her back and the swell of her bottom up flush against him. A perfect fit. He skimmed first his nose then his mouth along the juncture of her neck and the collar of her T-shirt.

Her breathy gasp at the sensation and the pounding rhythm of her pulse beneath his lips took him the short trip right over the edge of reason. His fangs ached so bad it was worse than a migraine, but he wasn't about to let them out to play just now. Not when she was so close he could sink them into the throbbing vein he saw. Everything in him wanted to feast on her. He leaned up on his elbow to get a better view of her face.

Her eyes opened halfway, their depths soft brown like melted chocolate and sleepy, and her lips curved into a sexy-as-hell smile. It was a damn good thing he didn't need to breathe. He wasn't confident he could have. What would it be like to wake up every morning with a woman like this, her perfect ass cradling his erection? A dream, only a dream, Slade sternly reminded himself.

Hell, there wasn't any chance she was interested in anything he or the clan had to offer. She had her own world.

She touched her cool fingers to his cheek. "You're still hot," she murmured.

Slade couldn't help but give her a teasing smile. "I know."

She shook her head, her forehead scrunching as if she'd been misunderstood. "I meant the fever."

Why was he prolonging it? Slade knew what he wanted. Feeding was out of the question. Clan protocol forbade feeding from a mortal who had not consented, but he could do the next best thing and kiss her senseless. Just to get it out of his system, of course. It had to be a symptom of the moon sickness, this insane urge to touch every inch of her first with his mouth, then with his teeth, then his tongue.

He tightened his hold on her waist, as his mouth covered hers hungrily.

Chapter 6

There were dreams one forgot by morning, and there were dreams that woke you with their erotic, pulse-pounding intensity.

The press of a hot, firm mouth on hers, the warm weight of a large hand slipping over her hip to rest low on her abdomen, shocked and surprised Raina. Her stomach quivered in response. Sparks skipped over her nerve endings, setting every one ablaze. She gasped at the sensation. No. Not a dream. She was awake. Wide-awake and fully aroused.

Slade took her slightly open mouth as an engraved invitation. His tongue, slick and warm, brushed her bottom lip then stroked in a sensual slide against hers. Everything within her contracted, then throbbed with longing. Her resistance melted into a liquid heat that flowed through her.

She'd watched over him all night. She'd taken off his shirt and tried to wipe him down with a cool wet washcloth to stem his fever, uncertain what else to do. It had been everything she could do to drag him into her tent once she set it up.

While she'd tended to him, she'd discovered Slade wasn't just handsome—his body was built from hard work and focused discipline. Old scars, raised badges of battles waged and won, were white with age. He was by no means as flawless as she thought vampires would be, which made him all the more real to her. She'd toyed with the idea of shucking off his pants, as well, but she wasn't comfortable going that far with him unconscious. At least not while she was awake. In her dreams, that was a different matter.

Having him wake up and respond to all the luscious thoughts of him that had been teasing her in her sleep was almost too good to be true. The kiss deepened and Raina twisted, wanting, needing better access to him. Her hands encountered the hot, hard smoothness of his bare skin just above the edge of his jeans. They moved up, slipping over the rippled edges of first his abdomen and then his chest as she made a slow, thorough exploration of his hard body.

He growled, literally growled, and the sound vibrated against her teeth and tongue. He pulled back, touching his forehead to hers, his eyes darkened with desire.

"Gods, you taste sweet." The husky quality of his

voice and the warmth of his breath against her mouth made a full-body shiver race over her from head to toe.

Her heart beat even harder against her ribs, her fast, harsh breath mingling with his. Raina couldn't get enough of him. Her breasts tightened and ached in expectation, the hardened tips of them plainly evident against the thin cotton of the T-shirt she wore. At this moment she didn't even have a bra on.

He nibbled kisses over her jaw and down her neck, his fangs softly scraping her skin as he went. Raina arched into him, moaning with pleasure. His hand slid beneath the edge of her T-shirt. The slight roughness of his hand rasped against her ribs as he caught her mouth with his and kissed her deeply. Raina squirmed, impatient and moved to give him better access. He cupped her breast in his hot palm, stroking the pad of his thumb across the pebbled tip. Her breath hissed out between her teeth as white-hot arrows of need shot straight through her.

Slade tore his mouth away from hers and rucked up the edge of the T-shirt she wore, exposing her breasts to the coolness of the air.

"Seeing as how you bathed me, it's only fair I return the favor." The warm, wet swirl of his tongue over her sensitized nipple made Raina arch. He suckled her, pulling her farther into his mouth as he cupped one hand around her bare lower back and the other around her bottom. Raina wriggled, unable to get enough, wanting him to touch the gentle, persistent throb building at her core.

"Can't let this one get jealous," he murmured, his

lips moving in a smile against her skin. The exquisite sensual onslaught shifted to her other breast, and Raina grasped his head with both hands, holding him there, a small moan of pleasure releasing from her throat.

Somewhere in the back of her mind her intellect screamed at her to push away from him and think about the consequences. Her body trussed up and gagged her intellect, then shoved it in the closet, telling it in no uncertain terms to shut the hell up, then blithely went back and enjoyed absorbing the sensations he stirred within her and demanded more.

He pulled back a fraction and stared at her for a moment so intently that Raina had the oddest sensation that he was reading her thoughts. "We should stop. You don't want this. Not with me."

What the hell did he know? She threaded her fingers into the hot silky hair at the back of his head, bringing him back toward her. "Says who?" The movement exposing more of her bare skin.

He swore, closing his eyes, as if in pain, his hand flexing against her skin, his body shuddering. He swore under his breath, and when he opened his eyes and looked at her again all traces of desire had been firmly erased, replaced by a cool, calm confidence. "Says me."

"Look, I'm not the one who started it."

"That's why I'm finishing it." He pulled her hand away from his neck. "We're still in unfriendly territory. We need to be out of here in ten minutes. Can you manage that?"

His sudden change flummoxed her and left her skin suddenly heated from embarrassment rather than desire. Raina remained silent as he grabbed his shirt and shoes and crawled out of the confines of the small tent into the cool morning air. She packed up with quiet, detached efficiency, growing angry with herself for throwing herself at him.

Even the early-morning birdsong seemed to grate on her nerves. As she tightly rolled her sleeping bag and shoved it in its sleeve, Raina realized that she was just as angry with herself as she was with him. Okay, being honest, perhaps more angry at herself.

She'd known from the first moment she'd seen Slade that he could easily get under her skin if she wasn't very careful around him. By the time she got out of the tent with her rolled-up sleeping bag, he was fully dressed and a good fifty yards up the trail, bent down on one knee, examining the ground.

She pulled the poles from the tent and quickly folded it, returning it to her huge hiking pack along with her crumpled uniform. He sauntered back toward her, his large body silhouetted by the first rays of the rising sun, his face a mask of concentration.

"Well, fever or not, you seem to be fully recovered," she said with a note of asperity. "What happened to you anyway?"

"Nothing out of the ordinary."

"Nothing out of— You passed out cold and had a raging fever for more than six hours! I was sick to my stomach with worry, not knowing if you were going to make it or not. And what would I have done with your body? I sure couldn't have hauled it all the way back down the mountain."

He shrugged, brushing off her concern. "I want you off the mountain. Today."

Raina narrowed her eyes. This was an about-face. He was not going to gyp her out of a chance to investigate these wolves. "Look, I only brought you here with me in the first place to help me track down these wolves. I am not going anywhere until I've seen them for myself. We're probably less than two miles from the cabin. As long as we've come this far, we ought to at least see my aunt. She might know more about these—" she paused for a second, thinking her choice of words through "—these creatures, than we think."

His eyes narrowed. "Doubt it."

She peered up at the filtered sunlight streaming in golden ribbons through the fir boughs. "I thought vampires didn't like sunlight."

"We don't," he said. He held out his hand. A dark curl of smoke appeared on his palm, then shifted to form into a pair of screw-you wraparound mirrored sunglasses. He shoved them into place, efficiently covering his eyes.

"You sure you don't want just to hang out at her place until we're past the midday?" she offered.

Slade shifted his weight. The offer was tempting. He didn't relish the blinding migraine that sunlight always produced. That, plus the moon sickness turning more virulent, wasn't the best combo for being in unfriendly territory. What had happened last night? He'd never passed out like that before. It was definitely time for a checkup with Dr. Chamberlin at the Clan medical clinic.

Perhaps that was the reason he'd been unable to keep his hands off Raina. Gods, she'd been all-out sexy. But when he'd heard her mentally berating herself, all bets had been off. He wasn't about to get into anything with somebody who didn't really know what they wanted. He'd learned from fraternizing with a few of the vampires and more than one donor that it led to bad juju on both sides. Better for him to concentrate on getting her safely out of here than on how her silken body would feel wrapped around his.

Since it was unlikely the Weres would make their move in the daylight, Raina would be safe enough if they left the area by the afternoon. He fingered the throwing stars in his thigh pocket. Good, she hadn't moved them. "Let's get there, look around, and then we'll get you back down the mountain before dark sets in."

Once he reached the cabin, he could transport back there later. It only took once for a vampire to visit a place to be able to transport there at will. He scooped up the handles of her fifty-pound hiking pack and his black bag with one hand and slung both over his shoulder. Not waiting to see if she followed, he headed for the game trail winding north through the trees.

Raina shook her head, mumbling to herself as she lengthened her steps to keep pace.

"Got something else you need to say, babe?"

"You vampires are a lot stronger than I realized,

which is why you passing out doesn't make any sense to me. Is there anything that actually harms you?"

Slade quirked up a brow. "You mean like garlic, crosses and holy water?"

Raina shrugged and nibbled at her bottom lip, which made him focus on that spot, wanting to kiss her hard and senseless. Now that he'd tasted what she had to offer, it was harder to resist. She'd ditched the stodgy uniform in favor of well-worn jeans, a soft brown hooded sweatshirt and a scoop-necked turquoise T-shirt. Her hair was a loose fall of dark waves over her shoulders and down her back.

It wasn't just staying out of the hottest sun of the day that was temping—so was the woman.

He focused on the trail ahead of them, looking for any signs the Weres were close by. "No. That's all Hollywood."

"So you're invincible?"

Hardly. She'd had his shirt off. Would have been difficult for her to miss the scars. There were enough of them. Invincible wasn't the same as immortal by a long shot. "I didn't say that."

"But if none of that stuff works and you're immortal, then—"

He caught her curious gaze. "But nothing. Silver can disrupt nerve and muscle impulses, leaving us immobile. A dead man's blood acts like a combo between a tranquilizer and a poison, and no matter how immortal we are, beheading or blowing apart a vampire is going to take them down permanently."

Her forehead crinkled. "Why wasn't any of that revealed in the media when vampires came out of the coffin a year ago?"

Slade knew she was talking about the nearly botched introduction of vampires to mortals that had started in Seattle. The transition of including vampires in mainstream society had been rocky at best. A year later there were still plenty of mortals who didn't like or approve of his kind.

But then, what did he care? Those people had never done anything for him, while the vampires at the Cascade Clan had given him a home, a family, a life.

"If people were looking for a way to take you down, would you offer up the secrets of how to accomplish that mission?"

She looked away from him. "Probably not. But there's a lot humans still don't know about vampires, and when people don't know things, they tend to invent something to fill the gap. Ignorance is not bliss in that case. It might have helped if vampires had shown humans that we have intrinsic similarities, humanize themselves so people don't fear the unknown."

Ah, there was the officer coming out in her. Investigate, probe, and demand the answers. He had to remember that while he was assisting her, she was still a mortal, and more importantly a cop.

He slowed his steps just enough that she noticed and glanced up at him. "In case you missed it, we're still human. Just not mortal, babe." Achilles had ordered Slade to help her, but he hadn't said *tell* her everything. The ancient vampire was more than just his commander. He was also the vampire who'd found him as a skinny, homeless kid on the streets, with no memories, no home and no future. He'd introduced Slade into the clan slowly, first letting him hang out at the safe house the clan had on the surface, then working cleaning and maintaining gear, equipment and weapons until he was old enough to decide if he wanted to train as a Shyeld, one of the human guards that filled out the ranks of the clan's security force.

Most people still didn't know about Shyelds. The council had deemed it classified information. Shyelds weren't donors. They weren't wholly vampires, either. They were highly trained mortal security personnel fed consistent small doses of ichor to amp up their abilities and senses, and they were able to live among and blend in with mortals. It was like being superhuman, which became an addictive sensation all on its own. Which is why Shyelds were carefully monitored and never given enough ichor to transition, unless, like himself, they were offered the privilege.

Slade had jumped at the chance. Hell, he didn't have anything to leave behind, so joining the ranks of full-blood vampires in the clan had been a no-brainer.

"What about you, nature girl? How'd you end up a game warden? It doesn't seem like your tribe is too enthusiastic about your job."

"They aren't. But then I think they would've been even more disappointed if I hadn't."

"Why's that?"

"Believe it or not, bad boys are my downfall."

Slade chuckled. "Yeah. I bet. Got to have someone to practice those cuffs on."

She gave him a cross look, but a subtle smile tugged at the corner of her full lips. "Do you want to hear this or not?"

"Hit me."

"College was my first real taste of the world away from Teanachee. I almost didn't come back."

He looked at her, so perfectly at ease out in the wilderness of these mountains, and really couldn't imagine her anywhere else, and certainly not stuck behind some desk in a high-rise downtown. "Why? You clearly love it and the people, and they like you."

"There was this motorcycle mechanic—"

"So now you've got something against motorcycles?"

"No. I love motorcycles. Especially big throaty ones."

Slade bit back a grin. Too bad he hadn't driven them here. It would have been a reason to bring his baby, a Harley-Davidson Softail Blackline, out for a run.

"But Rocky—"

"Rocky, this dude's name was Rocky?"

She turned on him, fisting her hands by her sides. "Gahh! You're infuriating, you know that?"

Slade let a slow smile cross his lips in a way he knew deepened the devil-may-care dimple that divided his chin. "You didn't seem to think so this morning."

"A momentary lapse in judgment."

He just bet. Under that cool, controlled exterior was a very sexy woman. He'd caught more than a glimpse of her this morning. All he'd wanted was to kiss her. But Raina wasn't the kind of woman he could just kiss and walk away from.

The day was growing warmer, causing the fragrant spicy-sweet blend of her scent to saturate the air around him. She was addictive. Slade tried to keep his reaction to a minimum when she pulled off her sweatshirt and tied it around her waist. He didn't want to stare at her form, but it was hard not to. The aqua color of the T-shirt that molded to her small, perfectly formed breasts deepened the dusky tones of her skin, making her seem golden-brown all over, and brought out the darker tone of her hair.

"How much farther?" he asked, trying to switch the subject.

Raina pulled her GPS from her pocket. "Less than a mile."

Slade took a deep inhalation, testing the scent currents in the air. The smell of mellow old wood, tar paper and wood smoke filled his nose along with the faint odor of Were—and blood. His shoulders tightened as he scanned the perimeter, searching for signs of the shifters.

"Shouldn't we be able to see it by now?"

She grinned at him, a slight bounce in her step, as she pointed. "It'll be up around the bend, just beyond that outcropping of rocks."

Slade glanced in the direction she'd indicated. Memory, like a shock of electricity, zipped hot across his vision. The shape of the rocks, the trees shorter. A wolf howling at the top of the rocks. A woman with dark hair and whiskey-colored eyes waiting on the porch of a cabin that looked like it belonged on the backwoods mountain set of a Hollywood sound-stage.

He smelled blood. Terror. Violence.

His senses amped to high alert, making his skin itch. His steps slowed as they reached the bend in the trail. "I've been here before. We need to go back. Now."

Raina was already standing ahead of him in shocked silence as she stared ahead, her mouth open.

The cabin, weathered gray cedar, even more rickety than his memory, stood with its rough-planked door ajar, hanging off one of its hinges. A dark smear of brownish half-dried blood trailed down the porch.

The air stank of the wet-dog stench of Were mixed with the sweet metallic odor of blood and the odd heavy sweetness of lilies. Slade bounded forward and, with a bruising grip around her wrist, dragged her into the brush. "Don't move. Don't even breathe." He cocked his head to the side, listening for the slightest rustle of movement. Anything that might indicate the wolves were still present.

It was late morning. Weres, like vampires, preferred the dark. But that didn't mean they couldn't be out and about.

Slade closed his eyes, concentrating all his efforts on hearing the sounds around them. Birdsong, the chatter of chipmunks, the bubble of a nearby stream. Then the low growl and yip and the slightest rustle of underbrush and the scattering of pebbles across stone. That's when Slade heard them.

"What do you think they want?" one Were growled low and deep to the other.

"Does it matter? Bracken said no one in or out until we know the vampires' defenses and finish growing our pack. Orders of the goddess."

"Bracken is a fool."

A yelp pierced the air. Slade bet someone had taken a bite for their opinion.

Raina stiffened beside him, drawing her Glock. *Was that one of them?* she mouthed, not making a sound. Smart girl.

Slade gave her a curt nod and put his index finger to his lips. Fat lot of good her gun would be. Without silver bullets, all it was likely to do was piss off a Were, rather than inflict any real damage.

Behind them the brush rustled. Slade propelled her forward, kept himself between her and whatever was coming toward them. There was no point in going in the cabin. The door wouldn't keep anything out and the walls would only act like a trap. He reached deep in his pocket and palmed a throwing star, then grabbed her around the waist and bent low. "Hold on!"

She flung her arms around his neck. Flexing his knees, he tightened one arm around her waist and jumped, landing with a thump on the mossy cedar shingle roof. Raina clasped his side tightly. She sucked in a sharp breath, finding herself atop the cabin.

From the brush and trees burst five wolves of different colors, teeth bared. The stiff ridge of hair along their backs was raised as they stalked around the cabin, two of them sniffing to the spot where he and Raina had stood moments before. Five against two. Not bad odds. Not good odds, either, but he'd take them.

"I knew I smelled the stink of wet dog," Slade said loud enough for them to hear. It was an intentional insult.

Chapter 7

Two yipped, two howled and the biggest one bent low and growled, his ruff of dark gray fur rising up around his shoulders and neck. The sounds of the leader warped into words. "We warned you once, vampire. You're trespassing. Now you, and your woman, will die."

Beside the larger leader, a wolf more brown than the others bared his teeth. "You killed my brother, vampire."

Slade flicked his gaze for just an instant to the brown wolf. He needed to keep his focus on the leader of the patrol. "He shouldn't have attacked me. You might want to think about that before you do something stupid."

The leader began to pace the front of the cabin, his

plate-size paws making no sound on the ground, his great brown eyes narrowing. "You vampires think you're so superior. But we've been here far longer than your kind. We are part of the land. Part of the people. And it's going to be ours again."

"Is that why you took Robbie?" Raina shot back in a series of growls and yips.

Stunned, Slade looked at the woman in his arms. "You know what they're saying?"

She gave a slight shrug, her eyes troubled. "I don't know. I guess so. I've never talked like that before. Maybe it's part of being the Wolf Whisperer."

The wolves' ears swiveled, as they glanced at one another with surprised uncertainty. The leader bent low, spreading his paws in an attack stance and bared his canines. "You dare try to take our Whisperer from us, vampire? This is an act of war."

Oh, shit. Not good.

Raina lifted her chin. "He's with me. I have brought him here."

The wolf leveled his gaze at Raina, his eyes serious and wary. "I am Tyee, called Ty, leader of this patrol. Why would you do this? Vampires are not welcome on our territory, Whisperer."

"To find you."

He sniffed the air, his black lip curling back over sharp white teeth on a growl as he raised the charcoal-colored ridge of hair on his back further. "He has already marked you. Leave him now and come with us, or you will no longer be welcome among us, either."

Slade was pretty damn certain he hadn't misheard,

but it was difficult to tell through the chorus of yips and growls being traded so quickly between the wolves and Raina. Marked? How had he— Oh, hell. The kiss. Of course they could scent him on her, along with her arousal. After spending a night curled up beside him, she probably reeked of vampire to them.

When Raina neither moved nor spoke, Ty turned to the others, his ears flattening to his skull. "Kill them both." Slade sensed some hesitation from the others. "Now!" the leader demanded, nipping at the two wolves closest to him, who yipped in response.

They hung their heads low and began to warily circle the cabin, ensuring that no matter where he and Raina tried to jump down, they'd encounter an oversize wolf.

"If you kill me, there will never be another Whisperer," Raina said. Her tone was confident even though Slade could feel her heart pounding against the wall of his chest. He tightened his hold on her waist and tried to transport them both back to Seattle.

The familiar pull centered behind his navel was more like a weak tug, then like a pathetic tickle. Damn. Either he was too weak from not having fed in so long, or the moon sickness was screwing up his vampire abilities, or both.

Time for plan B.

Only he had no plan B.

Double damn.

Slade took quick stock of his options. He had five throwing stars in his pocket. He could phase a blade if his powers weren't too on the fritz. He glanced at his pack, abandoned on the ground along with Raina's. He had explosives and weapons in there already loaded for Were. And there was always hand-to-hand. He'd get the living hell beat out of him, but he wouldn't die. Unlike the Weres. But he had Raina to think of. Her chances of survival from a straight-up shifter attack were somewhere in the neighborhood of nothing and nil.

"So be it," Ty growled. "A Whisperer who betrays her own is worse than none at all." Raina flinched, the reaction running the length of her body as if she'd been struck.

That pissed him off. He understood that they didn't want him here, but to discard her like a piece of refuse when she formed the link between them and her people was unconscionable. Their war was with his kind, not her.

One by one the shifters crouched, getting ready to spring. Anger and determination eddied in the air between them, making the hairs on his skin lift. Slade bounced his gaze from one to the next, not knowing who would move first, and shoved Raina behind him to shield her.

Two unleashed their coiled power and reached the edge of the roof, their hind paws scrabbling against the walls of the cabin, shaking it and casting aside loose cedar shingles in a clatter as they fell back to the ground. The third, however, made it a bit farther and pulled itself atop the small roof of the structure, but Slade was ready.

He threw a metal star at the wolf's face. It stuck hard in the temple, making it howl, as blood poured from the wound, blinding it on one side, but it kept pacing toward them. Slade wasn't taking chances. He used what power he had left to phase his bag onto the roof beside him, and took out the SIG Sauer loaded with silver bullets and let fly just as another Were scrabbled up on the roof.

The Were bolting toward them staggered back as the bullets ripped through his flesh. His anguished howl was silenced as he fell from the roof and landed with a thick thud. The wolf with the throwing star still lodged in his skull dropped off the edge out of sight.

"What are you doing?" Raina screamed as she pulled at his arm, sending his shots wild. "Don't kill them!"

He glared at her. "It's them or us. I pick us."

Slade shook her off and kept shooting at anything that moved. The wolves scattered into the trees, darting in and out between the massive trunks, and howling as they continued to circle the cabin at the tree line. For a split second Slade thought he caught a whiff of lilies and a glimpse of a blonde woman among the trees, as well, and momentarily stopped firing. He squeezed his eyes shut, then blinked rapidly. She was gone. Clearly the sun was distorting his vision.

Splinters of wood flew as he tried to track and shoot. He caught one shifter in the haunches. It yelped and went down, then staggered up and limped off into the undergrowth.

Raina's hand was small and hot on his shoulder. "Can't you just zap us out of here or something?"

"No."

"Just don't kill them. If we kill them we'll never find out what happened to Robbie. Please."

It was the *please* that did it.

Slade muttered some choice words to himself about women and soft hearts and stupidity, but he shoved the gun into the waistband of his pants at the small of his back and rolled his head, making the bones in his neck crack. "Fine. You want me to do this the old-fashioned way, we do it the old-fashioned way. But it still isn't going to be pretty. They're out to kill us, you get that, right?"

"Yes. But you're stronger. Aren't you?"

Slade gave one curt nod. "Damn straight, babe."

One of the younger wolves leaped to the top of the cabin. Slade bent his knees and waited, hands outstretched. "Come on, dog. We haven't got all day."

The wolf rushed him. Slade waited until the last second, then twisted out of the wolf's charge, throwing a skull-cracking blow to the side of the wolf's head and then a swift kick to its belly. The shifter yelped. Raina cried out. He ignored her, knowing she was safely behind him, a veritable vampire shield. Slade grabbed the Were by the scruff of fur and thick skin at its nape and rolled onto his back, flipping it off the roof with his feet. The shifter howled and fled into the trees. Three down. Two to go. At least the odds were now in his favor.

Behind him, Raina gasped. "You hurt it! I said don't hurt them."

Slade threw a glare at her. "You said don't kill them. Big difference."

From behind them a growl erupted as Ty sailed up and over the edge of the cabin's roofline straight in

Raina's direction. Slade shifted his stance, putting himself between them. In a split second he shoved her to the side as he caught the full brunt of the wolf's momentum, lifting him off his feet.

They slammed to the roof, a tangle of teeth and limbs. Slade gripped the wolf's neck in both hands, squeezing hard. Warm spittle flecked his face, and his arms burned as he held back the wolf's snapping jaws. The wolf's claws tore through his jacket and shirt. Slade cried out, hot stripes of pain searing across his chest and left shoulder as claws shredded his flesh. A loud crack ricocheted beneath his back, followed by a slow, low groan as the timbers in the roof of the cabin started to give way.

"Raina, jump!" Slade shouted a second before the roof collapsed.

Slade dropped, still trying to clutch the wolf's neck as they both crashed to the floor of the cabin. He lost his grip. For a moment his vision blurred as he saw double.

His shattered sunglasses hung on his face by one earpiece and the sunlight streaming in the now missing roof of the cabin made him squint as it started a hard pounding rush behind his eyeballs. But it wasn't nearly as bad as the red-hot pain blazing through his chest. The remains of his shirt were soaking wet with black ichor and he estimated that he had a broken left arm, several broken ribs and likely a cracked pelvis. Doc Chamberlin was going to be good and pissed when he showed up at the clinic in this shape.

Slade shook his head, trying to clear it from both

the onslaught of the pain and sunlight. He rolled to his feet, ignoring the pain that scored his back and stabbed through his eyes and into his brain like a hot knife through butter. Where the hell was Raina? Was she hurt?

The pile of broken wood and moss-covered shingles beside him moved. "Raina?" Slade staggered toward it, worried she'd become buried in the collapse. As he reached for it, the pile exploded outward as the lead wolf jumped out and shook off the debris. Slade pulled back and swore, keeping his broken left arm tight to his wet chest.

The Weres' second in command came through the cabin's open door, teeth bared. Together, growling their threat, they hemmed Slade in. *Well, like it or not, nature girl, these wolves aren't making it out of here alive.*

In one smooth motion, Slade pulled the SIG Sauer from the small of his back with his right hand and cocked it, holding it out in front of him aimed and ready to fire. "The lady asked me very nicely not to kill you, but either of you so much as sniffles, I'll blow your ass full of silver."

The wolves glanced at each other, some kind of communication he didn't completely understand passing between them. Well, well, what do you know? It seemed the Weres had mental communication powers like vampires. He'd have to share that little bit of information with Achilles, once he found Officer Ravenwing and got her off the mountain.

He pointed the gun at a spot directly between Ty's eyes. "What'd you do with the kid?"

"He's none of your concern, vampire," the Were growled, bright red blood dribbling from a gash in his side where it looked like a piece of wood had pierced between his ribs.

Slade popped off a shot right next to the leader's front paw that sent splinters flying up into the wolf's face.

"Wrong answer."

Ty shook away the particles of wood clinging to his muzzle and brazenly stepped forward a pace. "There are two of us and only one of you."

Slade turned and shot the second wolf in the shoulder. He crumpled with a yelp and a whine.

"Now we're even."

The large wolf flicked a gaze to his fallen companion, then back to Slade. Wariness warred with anger in the brown depths of his eyes. "He came to us."

"Right, and I'm fond of sunbathing." Slade cocked the gun, preparing to fire again. "Why are you stalking mortals? Why are you growing your ranks?"

Ty bent his head and closed his eyes, as if defeated. But rather than answer Slade, the wolf huffed. The disgusting sound of wet popping as sinew and bone tore apart to reform made Slade grit his teeth. Fur retreated, leaving behind smooth caramel-colored skin, and a shaggy mop of blue-black hair. But the deep, angry, brown eyes were the same as the wolf's had been when the mortal raised his head and the nasty gash on his side remained, streamers of red blood coursing down his bare flank.

He stared at Slade, his lips formed into a firm line. "I told you, vampire, we are part of the people. He came to us, to be part of the ancestors. If the vampires can walk among the people, why can't we? It is time we claimed what is rightfully ours and for your kind to go back to where you came from."

Slade was momentarily speechless as he stared at the man before him. Now that he was no longer in his wolf form, Ty looked like any of the citizens of Teanachee who might traipse into Jake's to buy a gallon of milk or some beef jerky. He was buck naked and built like a honed athlete on some serious steroids.

"So you're telling me it's our fault you're surfacing again after all these years?"

"Make of it what you will, vampire. But the time of the Were is at hand." He bent down to one knee, resting a hand in the fur of his fallen comrade, who whimpered softly, a wounded animal. The flow of yips and softly guttural sounds between them formed words Slade could understand. "Rest brother, I will carry you back to the den."

The Were's gaze shifted to Slade, piercing and intense. "If you are going to kill me, do it now, otherwise let me take my own and I will leave you."

"The woman is staying with me."

Ty's eyes blazed, a glimpse of the furious fire within. "So you *do* claim her."

Damned if he did. Damned if he didn't. Anything he said at this point regarding Raina would only make the situation more volatile so it was best to ignore the question. Slade wanted answers, but the double whammy of lost ichor and the sun at its zenith was about all he could take. He was weaker than he'd ever been and he needed to conserve what strength he had left to make sure Raina was okay, not argue with the damn shifter.

"We're not done with this," he warned Ty.

The shifter's eyes narrowed, but he said nothing as he scooped up the large wolf in his arms as if he were no more than a puppy, and stepped over the piles of debris to disappear into the woods.

Slade uncocked the gun and slid it back into his waistband, then staggered out of what was left of the cabin. He found Raina lying on the ground, unconscious, a nasty cut on her head.

The sight of the bright red blood, so tempting and sweet, sent a spike of hunger bolting through his system. It took every shred of control he possessed not to pull her up into his arms and kiss her there, just to see if she truly tasted as delicious as she smelled.

He kneeled beside her and lifted her into his lap with his right arm then gently patted her cheeks. "Raina. Raina, wake up. Can you hear me?"

Her head shook slightly from side to side and her lashes fluttered open. "What? Where am I?"

"We're at your aunt's cabin." He glanced over his shoulder at the ruin of broken timbers and roofless walls. "Well, what's left of it."

She sat up and put her hand to her head. It came back bright with blood and her eyes widened. "I hit my head?" She pulled up her shirt and held it to the spot, revealing her bra and golden skin beneath.

"Damn waste of fine blood," he muttered.

"Don't you even think—" Her words were interrupted by a gasp as she stared, then reached a trembling hand to touch the open gashes where the lead wolf had sliced him with his claws as they'd fought. He winced as she brushed over a broken rib.

"You're hurt bad."

He grunted, his body sluggish with pain and hunger. "Nothing a little blood and some stitches won't fix." He gritted his teeth.

"What got all over you?" She touched his tattered shirt and her fingers came away black with his ichor. His vision started to fade on the edges as the pain took over.

"Ichor. Vampire blood."

She sucked in a startled breath, her face contorted with shock then worry. "B-but there's so much of it. We've got to get you out of here."

"Just help me get the jacket and shirt off before the skin heals over it."

She swallowed hard and got to her knees, then looked around, her eyes narrowing and body tensing. "Where are the wolves?"

"Gone for now."

"And our gear?"

"Buried in that heap." He nodded at the ruined cabin.

Her shoulders relaxed as she gingerly pulled at the remnants of his clothes. "Not exactly the first meeting I'd envisioned."

Slade nodded. "And not likely to be the last." He let out a slow, hissing breath as the cloth pulled away from the worst of his wounds, where it had already begun to be covered with skin.

"Just hold still," she muttered near his ear as she peeled the shirt off his shoulders and back.

He grunted, then ground his teeth.

"Don't be such a baby."

Yeah, well, this wasn't like some ordinary bandage she was pulling off. He growled at her, showing her his fangs. "I've changed my mind. I don't need your help. See?"

Raina moved back around to the front of him and looked at the gaping wounds across the impressive span of his muscular chest. They'd already become smaller and, before her eyes, they began to scab over.

"That's amazing," she breathed as the scab fell away, revealing the raw new pink skin of a scar. The blackish blood around the wounds had dried to a thin crust, leaving Slade looking like he'd been smeared with ink or dark mud. While his surface wounds had healed she could tell by the glazed look in his eyes he wasn't fully recovered.

"We still need to get you cleaned up."

He shook his head, his golden gaze dark with pain. "Cleanup can come later. Right now I need to eat if we have a hope of making it down the mountain today."

She couldn't help her eyes widening in response. From the throb at her temple she could tell her cut was still bleeding. "You know I'm not on the menu, right?"

A corner of his mouth lifted in a half grin that revealed the longer length of one of his fangs. "You could be—if you wanted."

While logically Raina knew she should be terrified, she found instead she was fascinated. It made him seem more feral. The adrenaline rush from the wolves' attack was still circulating in her system, and rather than fight or flight, now that the immediate danger had passed, it was dulling her fear and feeding her curiosity. And Slade's revelation that her tribal ancestors were actually shifters had made her start looking at things from a whole new perspective.

"How do they work, anyway?" Raina reached out a finger and stroked the length of his fang.

A deep rumble vibrated through Slade as he closed his eyes. He grabbed her wrist and pulled her hand away. "Don't. Touch. That."

"Sensitive, huh?" she teased, but when he opened his eyes, it was her turn to gasp. His irises had turned the color of pale golden sunlight dancing on the edges of huge pupils dark with desire and need. They pulled her in, making her forget everything else around her, as if there were nothing but him and her.

"You have no idea." The rough pad of his thumb began to slowly trace a swirling pattern along the inside of her wrist, making sparks dance up her arm and spread through her system as he stared at her, as if she were the most beautiful thing on earth.

"Mmm," she murmured as her body seemed to tune itself to his touch. "Tell me."

Slade pulled her forward until her breasts were

pressed against the rock-hard expanse of his chest, and rumbled just beneath her ear, "I've got a better idea. How about I show you?"

Chapter 8

Slade knew what he was doing was wrong, but at the moment he didn't give a damn. The rules of the clan expressly forbade glamouring a mortal with the purpose of feeding from them without their consent, but the smell of her blood, strawberry sweet and sparkling with the essence of her vibrant life force, was too much for his weakened state. He needed blood. Her blood. Now. And her curiosity was consent enough for him.

He brushed his fangs in a slow scrape against her neck from the base of her ear down to the sweep of her collarbone. The path followed the thrumming beat of her artery that called to him like an addictive drug. With light, soft kisses he soothed her skin.

Small goose bumps rose as she shivered, an appreciative sound vibrating in her throat and up his fangs. "That feels wonderful," she murmured.

She had no idea how good it could feel, but he'd be happy to show her. Slade's fangs throbbed with hunger and desire. A light breeze stirred past her nape, lifting her hair and stirring the heated scent of her fragrance. Even as he sat this close to her, he could tell he was already shifting, changing to suit her most intimate fantasies. It was part and parcel of being a vampire, one of their many adaptations as a predatory species.

He kissed a path along her jaw and captured her mouth in a searing connection. Raina threw her arms around his neck and fisted her fingers into the hair at his nape. She pressed herself against him in an all-out assault. Her eager response inflamed the potent mix of hunger and desire ranging through him like a match to gasoline. When he pulled back, her lips were slightly swollen, the pink hue of them ratcheting up his desire to taste her to just under unbearable.

While he may have only been a vampire for less than a decade, he knew his response to her was far more than normal bloodlust. There was something about Raina that brought out the animalistic nature in him. It tempered his hunger with fear. What if he went too far? What if he couldn't control himself once he tasted her?

"Raina," he said softly, like a seductive whisper. "Will you let me—" he kissed her, a soft teasing kiss "—taste you?" The hungry edge to his voice went undisguised.

Even under a glamour, her own desire glowed about

her, drawing him to her. "Will it hurt?" she asked, her lips brushing back and forth against his mouth in a seductive touch that made his fangs throb.

"Just the opposite."

Raina slowly twirled the tip of her tongue over one of his fangs, in a hot silken slide that ripped through him from mouth to groin. Slade almost came apart at the seams. His erection pulsed almost as hard as his fangs in response to her. He hadn't been kidding when he'd told her they were sensitive.

The wet, soft heat of her tongue might as well have been curved around the tip of his shaft as his fangs, because he felt it in both places with equal intensity. He sucked in a sustaining breath, not because he needed the oxygen, but to maintain his control.

She pulled back slightly. A sexy-as-hell smile that stole away his ability to think curved her full lips. Raina crossed her arms, grabbing the bottom edge of her T-shirt and pulling it up and over her head in one fluid motion, leaving the glorious coppery skin of her torso bare except for the lacy white bra she wore that made her skin look even darker. Dusky nipples, barely visible behind the white fabric, peaked into hardened nubs.

He reached for her. Raina put a hand out on his bare chest, her touch like the licking flame of a candle next to his cooler skin. "I've got one condition, Donovan."

Hunger and desire were mixed in a lethal cocktail in his blood, demanding him to take what she offered. Gods, at this point he would have agreed to just about anything.

"You can taste me as long as you keep your hands to yourself."

Words were beyond him so he just nodded.

"Turn around."

He twisted to accommodate her. His ears picked up the metallic clink of cuffs an instant before she put it on his wrist and pulled his other wrist back behind him. Deep down an old memory raged. He been cuffed at least a dozen times before he'd become a Shyeld. But he'd never done so willingly like he did now.

He could snap the cuffs as if they were a set of kid's plastic toy cuffs if he wanted, but right now, if it made her feel better, he'd gladly put up with them. He'd do anything if she'd just let him taste her.

"This is just a safety precaution. It's not that I don't trust you, but—"

"You've never fed a vampire before," he finished for her.

A pretty blush deepened the tone of her skin and raw hunger gripped him hard. He watched as her long, tapered fingers pulled aside the dark sweep of hair, exposing her creamy soft skin for him.

"You know you're killing me, don't you?" he said hoarsely.

Her eyes glittered with delight. "My blood, my rules."

He leaned forward, using every ounce of his control to take it slowly—even as the hunger claimed him, every cell demanding he take what she offered with haste. Slade traced his tongue over the spot where her blood called to him, the warm shushing tempo of it increasing as her heartbeat grew faster with anticipation. Her skin tasted of saltwater taffy, sweet and slightly salty at the same time.

With ultimate care, he kissed her there, his fangs extended, letting her skin adjust to the feel of him. At the same time he let his mind take over. If he'd already broken a rule by glamouring her, what was wrong with going the whole way? He infiltrated her thoughts, allowing his mind to take her where she'd told him his body could not.

Raina gasped as he reached out with his mind and stroked his hands up her bare ribs, unclasping her bra and slipping it off her slender shoulders. She reached up to insure her bra was still there. Her fingers found fabric, but it didn't stop the sensations he flooded into her consciousness.

He mentally cupped her small bare breasts in the palms of his hands, softly stroking the silky, hot weight of them until the tips were peaked and hard. Perfect B cup, just as he'd thought. At the same time he slid his hands down her bare back, grasping her bottom, and sent clever fingers to tease the soft curls at the juncture of her thighs. His mind played other tricks, as well, allowing him to suckle her breasts as he also feathered kisses over her stomach and down the length of her spine. That was one of the advantages of being a vampire—one didn't have to touch physically to experience all the sensation. The mind was infinite.

"Are you sure you aren't touching me?" Raina panted, as she brushed her hands over the hard tips of her own breasts and patted herself down. "It feels like you are. And like you have several pairs of hands and maybe two or three mouths."

Slade pulled back and gave her a wicked smile. Every sensation he gave her impacted him, as well, and he was both hot and hungry for her. He could smell the soft, subtle sweetness of her arousal and her body was trembling. "Absolutely sure," he murmured as he kept twisting his wrist, rattling the cuffs. "See, no hands."

Raina let out a shuddering breath as he placed his mouth back on her neck and scraped his fangs in delicate circles on her skin while simultaneously he reached out to her and mentally traced the slick seam of her labia with his fingers, opening her and smoothing small slow circles on the hard bud he found there.

Raina gasped and arched at the sensation and his fangs sank slowly and smoothly into her. Blood, hot, sugary sweet and pulsing with sparkling life force, flooded into his mouth, making him groan. Gods above, she was far sweeter, more potent, than he'd imagined. Like fine aged whiskey, it hit his stomach in a hot, searing rush that left him light-headed, then spread a slow glowing warmth out through his body to his fingers and toes.

But in the fast, heated rush, he didn't forget she was tethered to him. With gentle insistence his mind urged her to open for him, and he touched her, his fingers sliding into her tight heat. Raina bucked her hips, bringing her up against him and the very evident, very real erection she'd caused.

Slade groaned and sucked hard at her neck. The pull caused a chain reaction in him and her, sending them both over the edge.

Raina let her head tip back as the heated waves of sensation overtook her, lifting her up, shaking her to the core, only to leave her breathless and boneless. His fangs slipped from her skin and he lapped at her neck. "You drive one hard bargain, lady," he muttered against her skin. "Maybe next time, I can touch you, as well."

"Next time?" Raina could barely breathe. Her world was fuzzy about the edges with a pleasant glow that suffused every cell in her body. She tilted forward and clung to him for support. "I don't know if I could survive a next time. That was—that was, wow. What was that?" she panted.

The slow, sexy smile that crossed his lips made her want to lick the indentation in his chin and kiss him hard. "That was how vampires feed," he said simply.

Suddenly the appeal of being a donor to a vampire made a whole lot more sense to her. She swallowed hard, trying to get her breathing back to some semblance of normal, but as hard and fast as her heart was beating it was an almost wasted effort. "They definitely didn't mention that on the six-o'clock news."

She swayed slightly, and he steadied her with his shoulder. "Are you feeling all right?"

"Oh, yeah. Better than all right. I feel great." Truth was she felt so relaxed and wonderful it was as though she'd spent a week lounging on some tropical beach with sugar-fine white sand and aquamarine water sip-ping sweet drinks with little umbrellas. She noticed that his eyes had returned to their normal whiskey color, but his fangs had yet to retract, the small points of them indenting against his sculptured lips. Boy, could he kiss a woman senseless.

She'd been kissed many times, but nothing, nothing could have prepared her for this. Raina wasn't exactly sure if it had been the kiss or the feeding that had brought on a full-blown orgasm that had rocked her socks off, but either way, it cemented her impression that Slade Donovan Blackwolf was serious bad-boy material who pushed all the right buttons in all the wrong ways. She gingerly stroked her fingers over her neck, finding small twin indentions in her skin where he'd used his fangs.

"How about you? Feeling more yourself now that you've had something to eat?"

Slade gave her a smooth smile as if he were reading her thoughts, and her skin tightened. "About as good as it gets until we get off this mountain."

She spread her hands on his bare chest, her fingers tingling from the touch. "We still need to get you cleaned up. There's a stream nearby." She grabbed up her discarded T-shirt, shook the fir needles from it and slipped it back over her head, then took a set of keys from her belt and unlocked the cuffs and tucked them back in the pouch on her belt.

Slade rubbed his wrists slightly, stood up, rolled his head back and forth, then phased himself a new pair of sunglasses. Together they started walking, Raina leading the way to the stream.

Raina glanced at him. "How can you stand to walk around in broad daylight like this?" She held back a slender tree branch in the path to pass it and let him catch hold of it before she let it go so it wouldn't smack him in his very broad, very muscular chest, which she seemed to be staring at way too much. His hand lightly brushed hers, sending a bolt of awareness zipping up her arm and down to her core. His gaze connected with hers.

"Feeding makes all the difference. Thank you. You don't know how badly I needed that." He sounded sincere, which made her tummy swoop. A bad boy who could be sincere was a rarity. In fact, she'd never met one before. The trouble with bad boys was they liked to have their fun, then be done. A luxury she would have loved to be able to afford, but that wasn't possible any longer. Not with her job on the line and her realization that the name of Whisperer held some real implications for her tribe.

"You're welcome." She couldn't hold his gaze any longer. Heat stole into her cheeks. She wasn't the blushing kind, but Slade had made her feel things no normal man had ever made her feel before, and certainly not with her pants still on. She wasn't about to tell him that the release had been more than welcome for her.

The burbling sound of water running over smooth stones grew louder as they neared the stream. "We're close. It should be just past those trees." The year-round stream had been the reason that Auntie Lee's forbearers had built their cabin near the rock promontory. As they cleared the line of trees, the afternoon sun warmed her back and changed the moving water into a ribbon of sparkles.

Raina knelt by the stream and motioned for Slade to join her. There was no point in looking for something to scoop up water. Their gear was lost in the heap of her aunt's cabin. Raina's heart gave a sad little lurch. "What do you think happened to my Aunt Lee?" she asked as he crouched down beside her at the stream's edge.

Slade brushed his hand, fingers splayed through his hair, the dimple in his chin growing deeper as his jaw tightened and flexed. "I don't know. But the blood on the porch wasn't human. That much I know for sure."

"How could you tell?" Raina scooped up a handful of water and smoothed it over his chest. The muscles flexed, whether from the icy temperature of the water or her touch she wasn't sure. She knew Slade affected her. But did she affect him?

"I could smell it from fifty feet away. It was deer blood. Your aunt is alive." He took a quick sample of the air, sniffing the old woman out. "She went toward town. Do you want me to track her for you?"

Raina shook her head. "We don't have time for detours. You're injured, and from what I just saw we've got bigger concerns." The dried crust of ichor began to dissolve, running in dark little rivulets down his sculpted, scarred chest and abs. She resisted the urge to follow the path of the dark water with her fingers. There was no denying the man was built. She scooped up another handful of the snowmelt stream.

A sly smile tilted his lips upward at the edge. "And the answer is yes."

Her hand stopped midmotion, the icy water trickling out between her fingers. "What?"

He grasped her hand in his much larger one, his thumb stroking the center of her wet palm, making her shiver. "The answer is yes. You affect me just as much as I affect you."

The shiver turned into a chill. Raina tugged her hand out of his. "Did you just read my mind?"

He tilted his head to the side and lifted his sunglasses with one finger so she could see his eyes. "Even if I couldn't, I would have known. It's written all over your face."

The sunglasses fell back into place and she suddenly noticed her reflection in their smoky mirrorlike surface. Her eyes were bright, her hair loose and full about her face, and her cheeks were a dusty pink beneath the smudges of dirt. The cut on her forehead was an ugly gash, still raw and weepy.

She scrunched up her nose and watched her reflection do the same. "Where? In between the dirt and the gash in my head? Maybe it was a smudge you misread."

Slade crooked a finger beneath her chin, bringing his mouth perilously close to hers. "I could get closer and try reading it again if you think it would help."

Raina swatted his hand away, mad at herself for being so damn attracted to him and mad at him for not letting her keep that bit of information to herself. "Are you sure I'm the only one who got hit in the head during that fight?"

Slade laughed, a full-out belly laugh that made her smile against her better judgment. He took his tattered shirt and tore off a piece, wetting it in the stream, and gingerly began to clean her face. Raina's heart did a little backflip at the tenderness of his touch so at odds with his bad-boy demeanor.

"Maybe I did hit my head, but that wouldn't change anything. You're more than you appear, Officer Raven-wing."

"I think you can drop the *Officer* now, seeing as how we've, well—" She waved her hand about. "Whatever. You know what I mean."

He stood up, then held one hand out to assist her. "So you want me to call you Ravenwing now?"

She took his hand and was surprised at the warmth of it. "Raina. Just plain Raina would do fine."

"You know, Raina," he said as he brushed her hair back and tucked it behind her ear, "I think I'm begin-ning to like you."

Chapter 9

Raina kept still, held her breath actually, like a frightened rabbit. He could tell she was waiting to see if he was going to kiss her again. Slade chuckled and kissed her on her damp forehead. He didn't need to read her thoughts to know she wanted more, but this was hardly the time or place. Besides, he was certain she was still under the influence of the glamour he'd thrown over her and that meant any reactions she was having toward him weren't purely her own.

She kept fairly silent as they walked through the woods, using her GPS as a guide. He could smell the way back, but he said nothing. If it gave her some security, let her use it.

Slade didn't know if her sudden quiet streak was because his admission that he liked her had made her uncomfortable or because she was still peeved that he'd read her mind. He shoved the thoughts out of his head and instead kept alert for the movement of anything suspicious. He wasn't taking a chance of them getting ambushed again no matter how distracting nature girl was.

A light breeze carrying the haylike scent of dried grasses and the woody scent of warm fir needles rustled through the tall tops of the trees, making the leaves shush and the trunks creak. Crickets and birdsong overtook the sound of the stream as they walked farther and farther down the mountainside, winding their way back to Joe Edgewater's farm.

Slade was frankly glad she didn't want to talk. While he wanted to just find a dark bit of shade to hide out in and wait out the daylight, he knew their chances would be far better if they made it off the mountain before nightfall.

In addition to the broken bones he already had he knew he was going to have one hell of a sunburn by the time they made it down the mountain. He did everything he could to minimize it and phased himself a leather jacket and a ball cap and some high SPF sunscreen. But beyond wearing his sunglasses and the hat, there was little he could do about the persistent migraine pounding away behind his eyes, as if it was slicing horizontally across his skull.

He limped slightly, the fractures painful although they were healing rapidly thanks to Raina allowing him to feed. Why had she done that? Was she just more susceptible to the glamour than he thought? She had no love of vampires, he was certain of that. Curiosity got the better of him.

"So, Raina, other than me and the shifters, have you actually had much experience with other beings?"

Raina climbed up a large fallen log in the path, then glanced back at him. "You mean do I randomly go around picking out weird stuff with which to endanger myself? No. Not really."

Slade couldn't resist the grin that tugged at the corner of his mouth as he leaned up against the log and rested. "Yeah, I could see how all this might be a little weird to you."

She brushed the back of her hand over her damp forehead and rested her hands on her hips, breathing heavily. They'd been hiking down the mountain at a pretty good clip, considering that he was still injured. Her eyes narrowed as her gaze raked over him. "You broke something in that fall, didn't you." It was statement more than a question. "You've been limping the last four miles and holding your left arm close to your chest."

"Few ribs, my left arm, might have cracked some other stuff, but it's healing fast. Should be good to go by the time we make it off the mountain."

Her face slackened slightly, but her eyes glittered with anger. "Seriously? Why didn't you say something! I thought maybe you'd cracked your collarbone or a rib when I was washing you, but I had no idea it was that bad. Are you sure we shouldn't contact someone to Medevac you out of here?"

Slade threw her a disarming grin. "Vampire, babe. You saw the cuts. I heal fast. But it's nice of you to worry about little ol' me."

Raina snorted. "You're a real piece of work, you know that, Donovan? I don't know half the time whether I like you or loathe you."

"I think you like me at least fifty-five percent of the time. That's more than half."

"Be honest with me. How badly are you hurt?" She speared him with a no-nonsense glance.

"Not enough to keep us from getting off the mountain before dark."

Her glance transformed into a glare. "That's not a straight answer and you know it."

Slade shrugged, his ribs protesting with a sharp pain shooting through his back. Teasing her came as naturally as breathing and it kept him from contemplating things he had no business thinking about. "You planning on reading me my Miranda rights before you interrogate me further, 'cause I'm pretty sure my lawyer would tell you I don't have to answer your questions."

Raina huffed, throwing her hands in the air. "See, this is when I loathe you. For one moment, just one moment, you seem like a decent, regular guy, then you have to go and ruin it by pulling this macho, I'm-such-a-strong-vampire crap. Why can't you just be honest with me?"

Her frustration and annoyance scented the air with a mix of stale sweat and smoke. Slade's face tightened, being able to smell her emotions only adding to the intensity of confusion. An unsettling combination of anger and attraction bubbled up inside him in response. "You want me to be honest with you?"

Raina shuffled her feet to move out of his way as he climbed up on the log beside her. He stared down at her, all broad shoulders and seething attitude, his eyes glittering like chips of cut topaz. "I don't like cops. They've done nothing but cause me a lot of hard times and try to cramp my style. But I think you're different. You're special. And I don't know why in the hell I'm attracted to you, but I am. In fact, if you weren't a cop I could see us hanging out together, having a few laughs. Is that honest enough for you?" Irritation was in his voice, but she could somehow tell it wasn't with her so much as with himself.

For a moment Raina couldn't make her mouth work. She wasn't exactly sure what she'd expected from him. A confession of deep inner longing? A need to feel alive that pushed him to these wild extremes? But not this. Not him admitting outright that he found himself attracted to her. A bad boy with a heart? Not likely, but she was dying to find out.

Temptation tapped on her shoulder just daring her. *You know you want to,* it whispered insidiously in her ear.

"So now it's your turn," he said, as if they were playing some juvenile game of truth or dare and expected quid pro quo. "Why'd you feed me?"

She sputtered for a moment. "You needed help," she said as if her actions were common sense, deliberately ignoring the attraction that shimmered like static electricity between them.

"I would have survived."

"That wolf ripped you open. If you'd been human, you'd have been… Never mind." She shook her head, refusing to meet his eyes.

Slade caught her hand in his, pulling her attention back in to focus on him. "You're right. If I'd been mortal I would have died from that attack. But that's why you're with me and not some other mortal officer out here. Achilles knew what these shifters are capable of and he didn't want you risking your life."

Raina quickly swiped her lips with her tongue. "You vampires are a lot more than people give you credit for." Deep down Raina knew precisely what had tipped the scales in favor of feeding him. Her curiosity had won the round, but it didn't mean she'd lost the battle. Not yet.

By nightfall they'd made it down the mountain. Slade took one look at Raina's compact car and decided a two-and-a-half-hour car trip cramped in that thing was going to drive him over the edge. Time was critical.

"If we drive straight through we could be back to Seattle by ten, maybe ten-thirty," she said. She appeared from behind the edge of Joe's barn where she'd changed back into her police uniform once more. She had it in her trunk along with some other extra items. "Here, I brought you a shirt."

Slade hadn't missed how she'd been casting glances

at his bare torso the whole time they'd been trekking down out of the woods. He purposely hadn't phased himself a new shirt; one, because the scars the shifter had left on his chest were still tender, and two, because he plain enjoyed goading her and the jacket was plenty protection against the sun on his back. "I've got a better idea."

"Look, Donovan," she said as she twisted her hair into a knot at the base of her neck and secured it with an elastic band, "This is my investigation and I'm too tired to argue. Let's just get in the car and get you back to your commander."

So much for Raina. Officer Ravenwing was back in full command. That was too bad. He'd really enjoyed walking with her when it was just the two of them and her officer persona wasn't hanging on like a third wheel. "All the better reason you shouldn't be driving. How opposed would you be to transporting back to Seattle?"

"Transporting?"

"The only way to fly."

Her eyes narrowed slightly with suspicion. "This doesn't involve you shifting into a giant bat and me flying on you, does it?"

He chuckled. "No. You've just got to hold on tight. Think you can manage that?"

A sexy smile curved her lips. "Why didn't you say so sooner?"

Slade was amazed at the difference in her attitude toward him. In the back of his mind he wondered if perhaps the glamour hadn't actually worn off yet. Perhaps that's why she was so accommodating. Perhaps that's why she thought she was attracted to him. Glamours were powerful things and she seemed more susceptible to them than most.

Being attacked by the wolves on that mountain had shown Raina one thing—she needed to live in the moment. While getting involved with Slade might be top on the list of really bad ideas for her long-term, in the short term it fell more on the list of what the hell.

As far as anyone else knew, she was doing her job. She was investigating the strange wolves and what had happened to Robbie. And if that meant she had to spend more time in close quarters with the seriously sexy Slade Donovan Blackwolf, so be it. After all, it was only temporary. And once this assignment was over, so would anything they shared. As long as she didn't let him totally distract her from her duty, she might as well live a little. After all, it wasn't like anyone from the force was going to be rubbing shoulders with the vampire community.

She stepped up close to Slade and wound her arms around his neck in a loose hold. "So do I have to do anything besides hold on?"

He wrapped a thick arm around her waist and pulled her close until there was not even room for air between the two of them from chest to toe. With her breasts pressed against the solid wall of his chest, all the air left her lungs and she couldn't seem to find a way to get a sip of it back. Being this close to Slade was getting addictive. Power rolled around him like a dark cloud full of sparks, shots of lightning igniting a storm of desire and need in her.

"You might want to close your eyes, just so it doesn't make you queasy." He gently stroked each of her eyelids closed, then ran the tip of his finger over her bottom lip, making it tingle.

"It's not going to hurt, is it?"

"Just a little tug. That's all."

A strong sucking pull from just behind her belly button yanked her inside out, leaving her weightless. The sensation like falling down the long drop of a roller coaster was so intense and so fast that Raina forgot to breathe. But Slade's arm around her waist remained strong and reassuring and in just seconds she felt firm ground beneath her feet again.

"You can open your eyes now." The amusement in his voice irritated her a bit.

"Just because I've never transported before doesn't give you the right to laugh at me." She pushed against his hold and he let her slip easily from his arms. She wobbled and he grabbed her by the elbow, steadying her.

"Take a few deep breaths. It should help."

"Should?"

He shrugged. "Kind of a guess. I don't breathe anymore, but I remember it helping."

"Great." Raina bent double, taking deep breaths, then straightened up and took a good look at where they'd landed. She hadn't seen the large airy atrium before.

"Where are we?"

"At the center of the clan's complex."

"I didn't see this part before. It's beautiful." The two-story room had a spalike atmosphere created by the pleasant, quiet bubbling of the water cascading down the stone wall on one end of the well-lit space and a zenlike rock garden on the other. In between were clustered conversation areas of cushy white sofas and chairs and a myriad of palms and other green plants. Overhead, soft light spilled from the frosted panes of glass, as if it were sunny just outside.

"Are you sure we're under the city?"

"Yep. About two stories." It hardly looked like something that should be underground beneath the bustling streets of Seattle. The complex was large enough she'd need a map, and even then she wasn't precisely sure she'd be able to find the security center where she'd first met Slade.

"So where to now?"

"Now we see Achilles. And tell him what happened with the shifters."

She fell into step beside him as he navigated his way through the atrium toward a set of dark wooden double doors. Slade paused, opening the door and holding it for her. "After you, *Officer*."

He'd seemed a bit irritated when she'd insisted on changing back into her uniform. He really had a thing against police officers. But she wanted Slade's commander to understand that she was here in an official capacity, not as her tribe's Whisperer, if she still even was one. If nothing else it made her feel more secure and capable when she was in uniform.

The hallway out of the atrium was far smaller and not nearly as well lit. One wall was of old brick, the other of concrete. All along the hallway there were shafts of light coming from skylights formed from small squares of glass set into the ceiling. Some were blacked out, others cracked, but they all looked old, with the odd greenish cast of old glass Coke bottles.

She stopped beneath one of the skylights. "Where's the light coming from? It's dark outside."

"Streetlights."

"We're that close to the surface?"

"Where we're walking used to be street level in Seattle circa 1889. They just raised it all when they rebuilt after the Great Fire."

Her people had stories of the smoke coming over the mountains. Great dark clouds that smudged the sky.

"This place is confusing. Now where are we?"

"How did you come in the first time you came to meet Achilles?"

"Through Doc Maynard's Public House up on First Avenue."

"And he met you there?"

Raina nodded. "Very cool bar with a fascinating Victorian vibe."

The devilish dent in Slade's chin deepened as he gave her a knowing half smile. "He took you down into the Seattle Underground from street side, then. That's why you bypassed the atrium. The doors we have leading to the underground are farther out toward the edge of the complex. That way we don't get any accidental tourists."

Raina's heart was pumping faster as Slade kept up the brisk pace down one hallway that branched into another and yet again into another. "How do you think he's going to take the news that the Weres want to crowd in on your celebrity status as local supernaturals?"

Slade's brow creased and a tic pulsated in his jaw. "They're just using it as an excuse to expand their territory. They don't give a shit about being recognized as legitimate. They've been perfectly happy for centuries to stick to their side of the mountain. Besides, what could they possibly want with territory in Seattle? It's not like they're going to go hunting."

"Unless they're bargain hunting at the Nordstrom Rack," Raina chimed in. But her joke fell flat with him, making her uneasy.

"Not funny. That Were said Robbie had come to them. If that's true then there may be some older kind of magic at work here that we're not aware of."

His words had the impact of getting slapped with a cold washcloth in the face. "Wait, hold up a second. Are you telling me you're blaming their abduction of a member of my community on *magic?*"

Slade shrugged and countered, "Are you telling me your tribe doesn't have any legends that deal with magic?"

Raina bit her lip. Sure they did. Plenty. And her whole life she'd worked diligently to keep that hocus-pocus mumbo jumbo from influencing her life. And now here it was, back again, taunting her, threatening to unravel everything she'd tried so hard to accomplish to bring her people into a modern world.

"That's ridiculous. They're legends. Stories. Myths."

Slade came to an abrupt stop that forced her to turn around.

"What?"

His golden eyes were intense. "A year ago we were just myths to mortals, too."

Raina nibbled on her bottom lip. She didn't like admitting he was right because it forced her to consider the possibilities that her tribal lore wasn't just lore after all. But then again she was working with a vampire. Against shape-shifters. She never would have believed that could happen a year ago.

"You've got a point. But that still doesn't help us."

"What does your lore say about the wolves and how the Whisperer is connected to the ancestors?"

Raina pressed her lips firmly together. She wasn't supposed to talk about it. Sharing that kind of information with outsiders, especially a *qelaen,* was forbidden. On the other hand, keeping it secret had done nothing to help her thus far. She sighed against the heavy invisible weight pressing in on her chest. Raina decided she might as well start at the beginning.

"When the Creator made man he put them into the form of Beaver to swim and be cleansed because the world was full of unpleasant things. And he gave the assignment of bringing human beings to life to four wolf brothers, who took Coyote's place as the head of all animal people after Coyote had cleaned up the place and then retired."

Raina pinched the bridge of her nose, her memory supplying all the smells of burning sage on the campfire as she'd been told the stories each year. "The four wolf brothers fought over what to do with Beaver when it was time to pull him out of the water. The Creator had told them they would have to cut Beaver into twelve pieces to create human beings. They all wanted to have the honor of being the one to kill it to start humans and made a bunch of different spears for their hunt. The youngest brother was the only one to survive hunting Beaver."

"They ever actually catch it?" Slade said as they passed a rusted-out bathtub and a brick wall plastered with old-fashioned Victorian-style advertising posters.

"Yes. The youngest wolf brother killed Beaver and cut it into eleven pieces that made up eleven of the tribes and used the blood to create the twelfth. Then he gave a piece to each of the animal people and had them scatter the bits of Beaver flesh and breathe life into them then showed the new human being what to do and what to eat."

He opened a door, holding it for her as they branched off down another hallway, this one without the small glass blocks in the ceiling. The hall was narrow enough that they could no longer walk side by side. "Sounds like your typical creation myth," he said as he stepped in front of her, leading the way.

Now the only view she had was his broad back encased in a black leather jacket and his tight butt in black camo fatigues. Not that she was complaining. It was an exceptionally great view. But if Slade was who she thought he might be in the legends, then this was the hardest part to tell him.

"It is. But here's the other part of it. The youngest wolf brother is our great grandfather, the one who brought us to life. And in times of trouble the ancestors return—those large wolves, Weres, shape-shifters, whatever you want to call them. The people will return to them, to become part of the ancestors and take on their powers."

"What, like some kind of homing device or failsafe?"

"Kind of, but not exactly. I think that whatever makes them able to shift is somehow dormant in our DNA. The virus you mentioned must somehow activate it. That must be why Robbie hasn't returned if he went to them."

That didn't make Slade feel any better about the situation. All it meant was there was another damn variable he couldn't calculate, and when it came to blowing stuff apart, like this weird situation with the shifters, it was all about the proper calculations. "Well, there's only one person I know of who might have a clue if that's true. Dr. Chamberlin."

"Dr. Chamberlin?"

"My commander's wife, Rebecca Chamberlin. She's a superbrain about genetics and DNA and all that. She'll be able to tell us if this is possible and maybe figure out a way to stop it."

"I don't know if you *can* stop it." Even Raina heard the worried edge to her own voice.

He slowed his steps and glanced over his shoulder at her. "What do you mean?"

"Well, there's this prophecy that one day would come a warrior not of the people, but born to the ancestors all the same. He'd be the one to end the line of the Whisperers and would come to rule both the ancestors and our people."

The odd, faraway look in her eyes made an uncomfortable swish in the pit of his stomach. "Why are you looking at me like that?"

She broke eye contact with him. Another bad sign. "I think that's something you should take up with your commander if he hasn't already briefed you."

A cold sense of dread sluiced down Slade's back. Damn. Double damn. This was why he didn't like cops. They knew what was coming, but were always waiting for you to fall into it, and then slap you for it.

He spun, blocking the hallway. It wasn't that hard— his shoulder almost reached wall to wall in the narrow confines and she didn't know her way back. She was trapped. "Why don't you just save me the time and tell me yourself. Obviously you know something I don't."

"It's just a guess. I don't know anything for sure," she hedged.

Slade crossed his arms. "But it's a good hunch. Good enough that Achilles believed you." The air around him spiked with the angry smell of pepper.

Raina bit her lip and nodded.

"Hit me."

"We think you may be part Were."

Chapter 10

The news was like a sucker punch to the solar plexus. Hard, deep, and if he'd been mortal, stealing his ability to breathe. "What the fu— Are you serious?" Slade rubbed a hand over his sternum and leaned against the wall of the hallway, letting the brick hold him up. "A shifter. You think I'm part shifter?"

They were twenty-five feet, maybe less, from the drab olive-green door leading to the security center, but suddenly it felt like hundreds of yards away. He saw the light of hope flare in Raina's eyes when she spied the door.

"I really think you ought to talk to your commander about this."

"Damn straight." He sprang into a stride, a sickening

mix of adrenaline, fear, anger and uncertainty pumping hard through him.

Slade marched the rest of distance down the hallway and slammed open the door to the security center. The head of every security officer sitting at a monitor or cleaning their weapon snapped up at the abrupt intrusion.

"Where's Achilles?" Slade said, the raw edge to his voice making his fellow security officers Titus, Mikhail and James tense. They traded looks with one another.

What the hell, man? Titus's voice echoed in Slade's head. Sometimes he hated the fact that he could hear them communicating, especially when they were all in the same room together. At one time, when he'd just transformed from Shyeld, he thought it was very cool. It had made him feel like he really belonged to the clan. Now, with all the emotion swirling in his gut it was a pain in his ass.

I don't know. Maybe his assignment was worse than it seems, Mikhail answered.

Nah. I mean, come on, look at her, she's hot, James said with a little too much interest for Slade's taste.

"The commander's due back in five," said James, his brilliant blue gaze roving over Raina. His mouth broke into a wide smile, showing off his fangs. "Hey, did you bring us lunch?"

An insane desire to clip James in the jaw streaked across his mind. Slade resisted it. "Can it, Crawford. This is Officer Ravenwing. We're on an investigation op and we need to talk to the commander ASAP about the Wenatchee Pack."

That sobered everyone up quick. A dark spiral of smoke formed into kick-ass Doc Marten boots, military fatigues and the broad shoulders of his commander. "What about them?" Achilles said. "I didn't expect you back so soon. Have you finished assisting Officer Ravenwing with her case?"

"We need to talk. Alone. Sir," he added as an afterthought, realizing how forceful his tone had become. He nodded at the other vampires on the security team.

"Clear out." Achilles didn't even have to look at the others before they vanished in spirals of smoky particles. He did a quick survey of the room. "I assume you're okay with Ravenwing staying?"

Slade nodded.

Achilles crossed his thick arms. "What happened?"

Slade glanced at Raina. She nodded, giving him the go-ahead to tell the story. "We went to the farm where the young man was reported missing. I scented Were presence on the place and we tracked it up the mountain. In the morning—"

Achilles furrowed his brow slightly and held up a hand. "In the morning? Why didn't you just keep tracking?" He glanced at Raina. "Were you too tired to continue, Officer?"

"No, sir," she replied, her chin tilted upward, her hands clasped behind her back, feet braced apart in a militarylike stance Slade could appreciate and loathed at the same. She wasn't the pushover he'd originally thought her to be, but she was still every inch a cop at the moment. "Mr. Donovan fell ill."

Achilles shifted his gaze back to Slade and he arched a single golden brow. "Fell ill?"

"Moon sickness, sir," Slade said quickly.

Achilles narrowed his green eyes. "How ill?"

"The usua—"

"He passed out cold," Raina cut in.

Achilles fixated his entire attention on Raina. "How long was he out?"

"About six hours."

"Six?" Achilles raked his hand through his blond hair, making it stand up in tufts and spikes. "This is far worse than we anticipated."

"What the hell did you anticipate?" Slade interrupted.

"I think Doc can answer that for you better than I," Achilles returned. He closed his eyes and Slade knew he was mentally communicating with his wife. Beside Achilles appeared another dark curl of particles that formed into a woman with curly chestnut hair, a pair of thick black-rimmed safety glasses on her heart-shaped face and a long white lab coat over her jeans and T-shirt.

"Glad to see you made it back in one piece," she said to Slade. She turned to Raina. "You're the game warden, Officer Ravenwing, right? I'm Dr. Rebecca Chamberlin." She held out a hand.

Raina shook it, but her expression turned pensive, as if she didn't want to hear whatever it was Dr. Chamberlin had to say. A sense of dread clamped down hard on Slade's gut, cutting it with cold, painful teeth. "Achilles says you know what's wrong with me."

Dr. Chamberlin looked at him, a flicker of interest in her eyes as if she were examining him under some damn microscope. "We believe the moon sickness you've been experiencing is symptomatic of exposure to the Were virus at some time in your past."

"I've never been bit," Slade protested.

"You're sure? Our records show that you didn't remember anything of your life before being introduced into the clan in the Shyeld training program. Is that true?" she asked.

Slade gave one nod in answer, but his mind filled with the first terrifying memories of waking up alone in Seattle, an eight-year-old with a torn-up foot. He was ten before the clan had brought him in off the streets.

"Then how can you possibly know what happened before you came here?"

"How do you know it's Were virus?" he shot back.

"Blood samples. You didn't think we took those for your physicals just for fun, did you? There's a form of the virus in your system, but for some reason it hasn't activated fully yet."

Slade speared his commander with a glare. "Are you telling me you knew about this? You knew I was part Were?"

Achilles jerked his head in Raina's direction. "She's the one who brought the intel to us about your mother's connections to the Wenatchee Pack. That's the first time we made the connection to it being the Were virus. We knew it was circulating in your system, we just didn't know what the virus was until she connected the dots."

Slade swiveled his blistering gaze in her direction. "At any time up on that damn mountain, did you think that maybe you ought to share this with me?"

She'd closed herself off behind her uniform. "Your commander determined it was need-to-know information—"

"And you thought I didn't need to effing know?"

Achilles growled. "You don't have to like it, Donovan. But you do have to abide by my decisions—otherwise, there's the door."

Slade swore under his breath. There was no way he wanted to jeopardize his place in the clan, but damned if he didn't feel every inch the outsider, just like he did his first year as a Shyeld in training. He'd busted his ass to prove his worth and now it was all slipping through his fingers like sand.

He glanced at his commander. It didn't make sense. Why, if they knew he was part Were, would they have allowed him access to the clan in the first place? "How is this even possible? I'm a vampire. I've already transitioned. I can't be Were and a vampire at the same time, can I?"

"Under the right conditions, anything is possible," Dr. Chamberlin said. "You just happened to hit the genetic lottery. An untransitioned Were made into a vampire. You must have been young enough that the Were virus was still dormant when you began taking the vampire ichor treatments as a Shyeld. From what I've been able to piece together, the Were virus is different from the vampire virus. It won't activate until after puberty, but the ichor would have arrested its development."

Slade thought about it. The wound on his foot had healed by the time Achilles had found him. He'd been recruited to be a Shyeld at twelve, far younger than the others because Achilles said he showed promise. He caught Achilles's serious gaze. "You didn't know any of this until after you'd already converted me. Did you?"

Achilles didn't have to say a word. His eyes told Slade everything he needed to know. "We knew nothing about your background until Officer Ravenwing brought us copies of your birth records and information about the tribe. Then there were some suspicions. Kaycee, your mother, had come to us seeking refuge. We didn't realize at the time of her transition that she was pregnant."

"Wait. Are you telling me my mother was some normal chick who got knocked up by a Were, then ditched him and became a vampire while she was pregnant?"

Dr. Chamberlin pulled her glasses off her face, folding them in her hands. "That's one way of putting it. We knew you had traces of vampire virus in your system when you came to us as a child. It's one reason you were selected to be a Shyeld."

Slade plowed his fingers through his hair, gripping the back of his skull. "Why the hell didn't anybody tell me that?"

"You didn't need to know," Achilles answered simply.

Slade pointed a finger at him. "I'm getting pretty

damn tired of that being a pat answer for everyone screwing with my life around here."

Dr. Chamberlin put a hand on Slade's arm. "Once we found out about the Were virus we didn't know precisely what might happen to you, given the unusual mix of genetic material swirling around in your body. We were being cautious, waiting to see if you were going to transition fully or remain vampire."

"So now I'm a goddamn science experiment *and* a security risk?" Slade pulled away from the doctor's touch and started to pace the length of the room like a caged tiger.

"Not yet, Donovan, but it's too soon to tell," Achilles said soberly. "No one else save for myself, Dr. Chamberlin, Trejan Dionotte and Laird Petrov have been informed of the specifics of your condition."

His *condition?* Slade stopped midstep and pointed to the door of the room. "Yeah, but you know as well as I do, the minute any of the other vampires in this clan find out, I'm going to be a second-class citizen around here. I'm a damn half-breed."

"I'm afraid it's worse than that. We don't know if the vampire virus arrested the development of the Were virus in your system or if there's still a chance given the right trigger that you could spontaneously transition," Dr. Chamberlin explained.

"You mean I could still turn into a full Were?" Slade pinned his gaze on his commander. A potent mix of anxiety, disgust and dread pinched down hard on his insides. "Will they kick me out of the clan if I transition?"

Achilles's mouth flattened into a firm line. "We don't know. This is kind of unprecedented. But the safe money would be on the council removing you as a security risk."

Freakin' fabulous. Just what he didn't need to hear.

"So since you're full of good news, I don't suppose you have any idea who my father is?"

Achilles's brow furrowed and a heavy feeling invaded Slade's chest, making his limbs feel like lead. "Hit me. This night can't be any worse than it is already."

Achilles's gaze flicked to Dr. Chamberlin's for a brief moment before connecting back with his. "We think the leader of the Wenatchee Were pack is your father."

Raina gasped.

Slade's knees suddenly wouldn't support him. He wondered who'd cut his legs out from under him. Hell. He'd been wrong. It was worse. Way worse. "Bracken?"

"Yes."

Damn. Double damn. He was on a roll of bad luck like an interstate highway stretching out before him with no stopping and he was on a turbocharged V-twin cycle from Hell.

"If the Weres find out, I see it going down one of two ways. Either they are going to force you to fight the pack beta for position or they're going to want to kill you," Achilles said.

The drab green of the security room walls swam before his eyes, making his stomach uneasy. Everything he'd counted on his entire life was falling apart like a cliff washing out beneath his feet and pitching him into a free fall. He glanced at Raina. Worry creased her brow, but she remained silent. He looked back at his commander and tried to focus on Achilles's face. "Why?"

Raina put her hand on his back and for a moment things fell back into focus. "When Bracken dies, you're the logical one in line to lead the pack. But in regular wolf packs the succession of pack leadership is always based on who beats the old alpha or who's the strongest if he has died. Since Bracken is your father, they'd expect you to fall in line. Their entire pack and its relationship to the tribe is based on ancestor worship. They'd never dream of you challenging and beating your own father. It would threaten everything for them. A half vampire half Were leader. Being a pack, they'd have to follow your command as alpha if you won, but they have no way of knowing if you'd command them to fall under control of the vampires."

He looked down at her. "Whoa. Back that semi up. Are you telling me I'm some kind of Were leader in training?"

"Worse. You're royalty."

Chapter 11

"I was freakin' born to lead a bunch of furries?" Slade swore and beat his fist into the brick wall of the security room.

Raina jumped back. A reddish cloud of brick dust settled over his dark shirt. The dust dissipated, revealing a large fist-size dent in the wall as if it had been made of soft white bread instead of rock.

She'd known Slade was strong, but she momentarily wondered if all the vampires in this room were just as strong. She'd been trying to stay out of their conversation as much as possible, partly because it wasn't her business and partly because she didn't want to get squashed like a bug if one or more of them got good and pissed.

"Get your head back in the game, solider," Achilles growled. "You going to tell me what happened out there, or do I drag it out of Officer Ravenwing, here?"

Raina took an involuntary step back, then corrected herself. It wouldn't do to show her fear, but her heart was pounding so hard it had taken up residence at the base of her throat.

Slade glared at Achilles, his expression full of anger and contempt, but his eyes were dark with deeper shadows of fear and uncertainty. "When I woke, we headed for a cabin Officer Ravenwing was familiar with in the area. We were going to talk to the woman who lived there."

"My Aunt Lee."

"And?" Achilles prompted.

Slade leaned his head back and stared at the ceiling, breathing out harsh breath. "The cabin had been broken into. Signs of a struggle. Partially dried deer blood on the porch and no old woman. The Were patrol had followed us."

Raina fixed her gaze on Achilles and he glanced at her. She added to the report. "They surrounded us and Slade jumped both of us to the top of the cabin and he fought them off, killing at least two and wounding the others."

Slade gripped the back of his neck with his hand. "The leader of the patrol identified himself to Raina as Ty."

"Identified himself, what the hell are you talking about?" Achilles roared. Raina thought she suddenly smelled a strong odor of pepper as if someone had just ground it in front of her, but it made no sense.

Slade's gaze flicked to Raina and for a second she felt as if they were a team. A team taking a dressing-down from a commanding officer, but a team nonetheless. Her heart swelled in her chest with a little bit of pride. Given the hit he had just taken with the news of his screwed-up genetics, she knew he needed her support but would never ask for it.

"She's a Wolf Whisperer, sir. Able to communicate by some kind of genetic bond with them. Something about her tribal connection."

Achilles turned on her, advancing at a pace that had her scrambling backward until her back hit a brick wall, scared enough to jump out of her skin. She'd been unprepared for his reaction. "Is this why you came to us, to infiltrate our security, to lead him right into their hands?"

"No!" Raina yelped.

His wife shook his arm. "Achilles! Think. She's a mortal officer of the law, not a shifter," she said, her voice edged with warning.

Slade gripped Achilles's shoulder in a clear signal to back off. "She thought it was a bunch of tribal mumbo jumbo until she actually talked to the things."

Achilles whipped his head around. "She can talk with them, too?"

"Yeah, better than I can."

Achilles's shoulders slackened. "*You* can talk to them? When were you planning on divulging that bit of information?"

"I didn't realize that's what it was. Out on patrol, I could hear them talking in the woods, but I just figured it was some kind of vampire tracking thing, just like the mental telepathy we have. I didn't realize I was hearing shifters."

The harsh planes of Achilles's face visibly relaxed. Raina inched away from the wall. "So what were they saying?"

"They figure since we started the whole coming-out party with the mortals, they have a right to join in."

The corner of Achilles's mouth quirked up in a semismile. "Is that their plan? Gain enough numbers, then overwhelm us?"

Slade gave him a slight smile in return. "Sounds like it, sir."

Achilles let out a bark of laughter and clapped a hand on Slade's shoulder so hard it made Slade huff out a breath. Both of them looked way too pleased, in Raina's opinion, cocky even. "Well, that's the best news I've had all night."

"How's that?" Dr. Chamberlin asked.

Achilles turned to her. "If this is just a pissing contest over territory, vampires are way more appealing to mortals than Weres. We've got victory locked in."

Dr. Chamberlin threw her husband an arch look that told him he was too confident for his own good.

Slade cleared his throat. "There's one more thing, sir."

The half smile on Achilles's face faded. "Why does it sound like something I don't want to hear?"

"I think I spotted Eris out in the woods running with the Were patrol. It's just a hunch, but I did hear the Weres mention the word *goddess*."

Achilles let loose a string of curses that almost turned Raina's hair blue. Dr. Chamberlin's face looked suddenly drawn and tight. Oh, this was bad. Very bad.

"Are you sure?"

"Yes."

"Who's Eris?" Raina asked.

All three vampires turned and stared at her as if she'd just rolled off the tailgate of a turnip truck.

"Eris, daughter of Ares, is the bitch goddess of chaos," Achilles said through gritted teeth. "And if she'd got a finger in this, you can be sure it won't turn out well for anybody, especially the mortals."

Raina stared at the three vampires crowded with her into the confines of the small, slightly musty Cascade Clan security briefing room two stories under the streets of Seattle. Achilles, Dr. Chamberlin and Slade all looked seriously uptight about this Eris character joining the battle shaping up between the Weres and the vampires. Raina found it somewhat amusing that they could get so worked up over some ancient Greek goddess. Personally, she thought they had a lot bigger things to be concerned over.

"Are you talking like ancient Greek mythology, minor goddess, Eris? The one who likes to throw the golden apple of discord around to stir up trouble?" she asked.

"The same," Achilles said, his face deadly serious. The artificial glow from the myriad of flat-screened computer monitors in the room only made him look more ominous.

"You've got to be kidding me. You powerful vampires are afraid of a mythical goddess?"

"Not mythical. Which you'd know if you'd ever met her," Slade said darkly.

Raina shook her head. "Of course I haven't. She doesn't exist."

"That's why you're not scared," Slade said with absolute certainty that sounded to Raina like it came from personal experience. The frenzied look in his eye confirmed it. "I've met her. Trust me, you ever run up against her, you'll know why she's a threat. DMDs won't even take her down."

"DMDs?" Raina asked.

"Dead Man Darts," supplied Dr. Chamberlin. "Tranquilizer darts filled with dead man's blood will take out a vampire for hours. It's a swift-acting poison in their systems, rather like what would happen if you shot them up full of liquid nitrogen. I watched a whole barrage of them pass right through her as if she was a hologram."

Dr. Chamberlin slipped her safety goggles back in place, then grabbed hold of Achilles's bicep. "If you're thinking of sending Slade and Officer Ravenwing back up that mountain in Were territory with Eris on the loose, then I need to get back to my lab and see if I can come up with something that might stabilize his condition further."

"How long would that take?" Slade asked.

"Forty-eight hours, give or take. I've been working on something but I want to finish testing it first."

Achilles pinned Slade with a no-nonsense look.

"You've forty-eight hours before I want you to report back for duty."

Slade stood a little straighter. "What's the plan?"

"We need more information. We need to know when they plan to strike. Whatever they are going to do is going to be splashy. Being subtle isn't exactly in their nature."

"Yes, sir." Slade saluted Achilles by placing his fist across his chest and bowing his head slightly.

"And Donovan—"

His head popped up. "Sir?"

"Keep an eye on Officer Ravenwing while she's our guest here at the complex. With her connected to the clan in this operation it's not safe for her to be without backup."

Raina bristled. She wasn't staying here to just wait around. She needed to report in to the station. "I have backup. My whole depart—"

Achilles cut her off with a dark look. "With all due respect, they aren't vampires, Officer. They won't know how to fend off a Were attack should one show up unexpectedly."

"I think I'd notice a huge wolf headed my way."

"And what about an ordinary man in a business suit? Or a kid in jeans and a hoodie? How about a young mother in a park? Would you suspect *them,* too?" he countered.

Her brow furrowed with confusion at his question.

"Because that's precisely what a shifter would look like just before they attacked you, and you'd never even suspect them. Donovan has a nose for this. You don't.

Do us all a favor and stick together and stay vigilant. I want you both able to report back here in forty-eight hours."

Raina nodded, but Slade noticed the rebellious look sparking in the brown depths of her eyes. He was going to have to stick closer to her than a pair of leather riding chaps if he wanted to make sure she didn't get into anything she couldn't handle. She might be a trained police officer, but he knew damn well that there was no training available to mortals on handling the kind of storm they'd wandered into.

Achilles and Dr. Chamberlin took each other's hand and vanished into a spin of dark particles.

Raina shook her head. "I don't know if I'm ever going to get used to you vampires doing the genie, smoke-and-mirror thing."

Slade could tell it wasn't the transporting that agitated her—she was badly shaken by what Achilles had said. He put a hand on her shoulder and gave her a light and easy smile, trying to reassure her and find a way to take her mind off Achilles's accurate but unsettling warning. "You actually did really well on your first transport. Want to see something else cool?" He fluxed, turning invisible.

She jumped back slightly, then spun around, looking for him. "Slade? This isn't funny. Where are you?"

He phased through the wall of the security room, the shift in his particles passing through the solid structure of the wall feeling a lot like walking through thick-set gelatin. Fluxing back into his visible form, he opened the door from the other side on a shocked Raina.

"How'd you do that?"

"Fluxed. Told you it was cool."

Raina walked through the door he held open for her and joined him as they headed back in the direction of the main complex. "Now you're just showing off," she said without heat. He was glad she'd gotten her spunk back.

"There's a lot more to being a vampire than you're aware of. Same goes for the Weres. What you've seen is just the surface. I know you don't like being kept here, but it really is for your own safety."

Raina swept a loose strand of her dark hair that had escaped her severe bun, confining it behind her ear. "So what do we do now? Shouldn't you get that broken arm looked at?"

"No point. It's practically healed. We're going to sit down, put our heads together and come up with a plan." They walked in companionable silence through the maze of hallways leading back to the atrium. He was grateful she was not the kind of woman who needed to run her mouth just to fill in a stretch of quiet. It gave him time to think.

A Were-vampire turf war was one thing. A turf war handcrafted by the goddess of chaos was quite another.

Slade had seen for himself the kind of confusion, desperation and fear she loved to cause. She didn't care who was hurt or in turmoil as long as someone was. She lived on aggression, torment and disruption—literally inhaling it. Just thinking of the last time he'd come up against the goddess when he'd been backup for Achilles on a raid of a genetics lab creating a deadly vampire vaccine made his skin turn ice-cold.

"The only way we're going to get anywhere with this is if we figure out what they want," Slade muttered, more to himself than to Raina.

"They want to be recognized by humans."

Slade grunted. "That's what they say, babe. That's not what they mean." There were three things Slade knew for sure. One was that Weres needed a strong leader. He seriously doubted it was some older alpha pushing them to expand the territory. Two, whatever happened, he was a half-breed, part Were, part vampire. That meant at some point the vampires might not want him in their clan, but the Weres weren't going to welcome him, either. And three, the Weres weren't going to stop with just making themselves known to mortals. They wanted power, and coming out was just the beginning.

"So what's your plan, hotshot?" Raina asked, breaking the silence.

"We're going to capture one of them and bring him back here."

Raina pulled up short, forcing him to stop. "To the clan complex?"

Slade nodded slowly, the plan beginning to gel in his brain. "We bring him back and Achilles and I get him to talk."

"Then it has to be the right wolf. Not just any Were will do. You get one that's too far down the hierarchy in the pack and they won't know anything."

"Exactly."

"So who do you have in mind?"

"Ty."

Raina crossed her arms, making the epaulets on the shoulders of her uniform buckle a bit. "You can't be serious."

"Why not? If they trust him to lead a patrol that large, he'll know what's going on."

"He hates you."

Slade's lips twitched with amusement. "They all do, babe. Vampire, remember?"

Raina pressed her fingers to her temples, rubbing them in small circles. "This is the craziest plan I've ever heard of." He noticed the dark smudges forming beneath her eyes. It was nearly three in the morning. She had to be beat. He needed to get her to a place where she could sleep.

"Little C4, a few charges, some wire, we can knock down the side of a mountain, let alone a Were."

"Is that your solution? If you can't fix it, blow it up?"

Slade shrugged. "Works for me."

She groaned out her frustration. "And how are you planning to get Ty into this clever trap of yours?"

Slade's jaw popped as he worked it back and forth. He hadn't considered what he'd have to do to get Ty's attention. He kind of figured just strolling onto Were territory would be enough.

"You could use me as bait," she suggested.

His gaze locked down hard on hers. "No." He lengthened his stride, as if putting distance between them would make the idea go away, but the soft feminine scent of her had invaded his senses, making him all too aware of how very mortal and fragile she was, no matter her determination or training. One hard hit from a Were and she was dead. Simple as that. And that was not going to happen. Not on his watch.

"But they—"

"No."

"I coul—"

"No."

Raina came to a dead stop in the hallway and he was forced to turn around. Her hands were wedged on her hips and her feet spread apart, looking every inch the police officer who wasn't used to taking no for an answer. "Look, Donovan. We don't have a lot of options here. They don't want you. They want me. I'm their Whisperer and if they think I've defected to their side, they'll be all over it. I'm not just good bait. I'm perfect bait and you know it."

"No."

She marched toward him, the planes of her face catching the shifting shadows between one artificial light and the next suspended along the hall. Determination had hardened her features, her gaze, as she stared into his face. Slade second-guessed himself. Maybe he actually preferred her frightened instead of no-guts-no-glory bold and willing to put herself in danger to help others.

"What other options have you got? Roll into Were territory Rambo style and hope you don't have to shoot through them all to get to Ty?"

The corner of his mouth tipped up in a bad-boy smile that made her heart double-bump hard in her chest. "That does sound appealing," he said.

Raina punched him in the arm, pissed off at both her irrational attraction to the man and his irrational refusal. She was the most logical choice to tempt the Weres, in particular Ty, into a trap. It made sense. Why fight it? "Get real, Donovan. You want this Were or what?"

The smile faded, replaced by an expression of sheer determination that knitted his dark brows together in a firm line. "Yeah. He's the one I want."

"Then let's do this."

"I don't like it."

Raina grinned at him. "I think I can handle it. Officer, remember?"

He deliberately ignored her comment, and turned to walk away. "We've got a plan, now we need to get you to a bed."

She raised a brow. "Wow, that was smooth. You always sweet-talk ladies that way?"

Slade spun on his heel, leaning in close enough to her that his body heat seeped through her clothes. His face was hard, and a little bit frightening, giving her a glimpse of the darkness lurking just below the surface.

He put one hand on the wall just beside her head. His sensual lips curved into a sexy-as-hell grin that really did make her knees suddenly unstable. "As tempting as that sounds—" he raked her with a red-hot gaze that made her breasts tighten in response "—I'm worried that you're going to fall over if you don't get some sleep. Being sleep deprived makes you an easier target."

"For you or for the Weres?" she teased, her tone just this side of breathless.

"Both," he shot back, not to be outdone.

Raina brushed her hand over her forehead, where a headache was starting to throb behind her right eye. Now that Slade had mentioned it, she was bone tired and her eyes were gritty. Sleep couldn't hurt and it might actually help. "Fine, whatever. I don't suppose your commander would consider letting me stay in a hotel nearby."

"Nope."

"Great."

"He said to keep an eye on you, which is precisely what I plan to do."

She crossed her arms. "You are *not* watching me sleep."

He grinned. "You're welcome to try and stop me, but I think you're going to be dead to the world once you hit the sheets."

"So where are you taking me?"

"My place."

Chapter 12

He didn't ask. Instead, Slade grasped Raina about the waist, bringing them together in full-body contact that made her skin contract over her bones and her breasts ache. "No point in making you walk the remaining sixteen blocks to the living quarters."

She didn't even get time to protest before the hallway outside the clan security room turned into a swirl of light and dark and she was tugged backward by an unseen force. Raina shut her eyes tight and clung to him.

As soon as the unsettled, floaty sensation that transportation caused settled down again, she opened her eyes and pushed away from him. She stepped cautiously into his private realm, taking it all in—clues to the man he really was.

They were in an upscale apartment that was part bachelor pad, part garage. The entryway looked partially into his living room, where she spied a black leather recliner and the glass edge of a coffee table. The floors were dark wood.

Rather than windows, the plain white walls sported enormous blowups of full-color pictures of various scenic sites around the Pacific Northwest. Mount Rainer, the ancient volcano, with its ever-present cap of glacial white, a stretch of tree-rimmed coastline littered with monolithic rocks out in the water like enormous stone haystacks, and a forest path winding into the mists through a stand of ancient old-growth timber heavy with moss on the massive lower branches.

"Funny. You don't seem the outdoorsy type." She turned her gaze away from the pictures for a second. He was standing beside her, a warm and solid presence, but not touching her. That didn't stop the vibration of the air between them.

"I'm not. Just find it soothing. I haven't been a vampire long enough to feel comfortable with the lack of windows down here."

"When did you become a vampire?"

"When I was twenty-five."

"But you've been here longer than that."

He nodded. "Yeah. They took me in when I was ten. I'd been living on the streets for two years."

"You were homeless?"

Slade cupped the back of his neck with his hand. "Yeah. But it taught me a lot."

Raina was surprised at how casual he sounded. It

had to have been incredibly traumatic to be a small kid alone and homeless in a big city.

"Why didn't they just transition you when they found you?"

"The clan has pretty strict rules about transitioning kids. They took care of me, then let me serve as a Shyeld first, starting when I was twelve."

"Shyeld?"

"Mortal security officer pumped up on vampire ichor."

"But you were just a little kid."

Slade dropped his hand and shrugged. "I didn't mind. Being on ichor in small doses like that makes you feel like you're a superhero. All of a sudden you can do things most kids your age only watch on cartoons. You can see things far away, you can jump and run faster than anybody else and you're strong. And—" he winked at her "—the girls can't resist you."

Raina shifted uncomfortably. Knowing how the feeding had made her feel, she could only imagine how taking the ichor might work. It would be every teen boy's fantasy. No wonder he'd never questioned his decision or given a damn where he'd come from. If she'd felt thrown away, she never would have looked back, either. "That's what Dr. Chamberlin was talking about."

"Yep. The clan is pretty much the only thing I've ever known."

Raina could suddenly see how news about his Were heritage would have been even more disturbing. It would be like finding out you were adopted and had been lied to your whole life. Everything you'd come to rely on as reality would shift like unstable sand beneath your feet. No wonder he held such contempt for the Wercs. They threatened his connection to the only home and family he'd ever known.

She glanced at his coffee table, a twisted, bleached piece of driftwood, the mangled roots of a tree at one time, spreading out from a thick base and topped with a glass oval. On top of it was a spread-out newspaper with what looked like engine parts on it and a couple of tools neatly lined up.

Slade might look like a bad boy, might even talk and act like one, but he had layers. A bad boy to the core didn't give a damn at the mess he left behind; he lived totally in the moment. The precision and order in how the tools were set up and the engine parts arranged said there was part of him that craved order and rules.

On the other hand, in the far corner, where a normal person might have had a couch to go with the recliner was a huge flat-screen TV bolted to the wall and a Softtail Harley Davidson motorcycle, low, black and mean-looking. Raina's breath caught for a second, then she felt compelled to touch it. The black paint seemed to shift in color, sometimes glowing with a deep amethyst, sometimes with a royal-blue, and the chrome on the dual exhaust pipes and engine block had been lovingly polished to a mirrorlike sheen.

"That's my baby." Slade's voice held a note of pride as he leaned his large shoulder against the wall, crossing his arms.

Raina slid an appreciative hand over the arc of the

thick chrome handlebars and saw her distorted reflection mirrored in the enormous exhaust pipes. He took exquisite care of his bike. "Nice."

"If I'd known you like to ride, we could have taken this up to Teanachee instead of your car."

Raina couldn't keep herself from smiling. She nibbled on her bottom lip. "We still could." She slid to straddle the bike and sighed, then glanced at him.

Slade's tawny eyes smoldered. "You'd look good on it."

A spark of awareness arced in the air between them, causing a shiver to dance along her skin. His gaze was mesmerizing, sucking her in, making her want to snuggle up to his bare chest the way she'd done in the tent. "It's a growler, isn't it?"

"I was thinking more of a screamer. But, yeah, that works too."

Her gaze flicked to the recliner. "That where you sleep?" She knew she was playing with fire and she didn't care. The uneasy chemistry simmering between her and Slade was slowly morphing and changing into something far more dangerous and sexual.

He grinned, pushing off the wall, moving toward her. Despite his size, his movement was sensual and fluid. "No, but I'd be happy to give you a tour."

"Of your recliner?" she teased.

He stepped around her, growing closer like a wolf circling its intended target, moving slowly and deliberately in on her space, stealing her air. His eyes glittered with golden promise. "Where I sleep."

Suddenly, Raina's mouth felt very dry, and her pulse

was hammering hard. Maybe sleep was highly over-rated.

"Vampires sleep?" She sounded a little breathless. But then looking at a man like Slade, who wouldn't be?

He grinned. "Usually only during the daylight hours and only if there isn't something more interesting to do." He jerked his head to the side. "Come on, as long as you're bunking here I might as well give you the dollar tour."

He strolled past her, filling the air with a mix of leather and cedar that made her inhale deeply. Raina fell into step behind him. They went into the kitchen. It was sparse, just like hers. The black granite was shiny under the overhead lights and the dark cherrywood cabinets made it look more upscale than her apartment. In the center was an island with three bar stools. She didn't have time to cook; in fact, she wasn't even sure she'd used her stove in the past month. If it couldn't be microwaved, eaten fresh or quick heated over a camp stove, she didn't bother with it. "Nice. Looks like you don't use it much."

"Liquid diet means I don't have a reason to cook much," he said with a wicked smile.

The tour took a turn out of the kitchen into a small dining room that contained a home office rather than a dining-room table and chairs.

"I take it you don't entertain that often, either?" she said, gesturing to the computer with a three-screen setup and rack of DVDs beside it.

"If I'm going to hang out with friends, we usually go out to eat."

Her hand slipped lightly over her neck, where his lips and fangs had touched her. She could only imagine what kind of places they liked to go out to catch a bite. "Where do you go? The local blood bank?"

He chuckled, the smile touching his lips, curving them into a sexy-as-hell smile that made her tighten all over. "Funny. Nah, I'm young enough I prefer the live stuff. Believe it or not, it's not too difficult for me to find a willing donor or two."

She'd bet.

"Let me show you the rest of the place."

As they walked down the hall, she followed behind him, admiring his broad back, narrow hips and fantastic butt.

He cruised past the half bath in the hallway, jerking his thumb at a darkened, half-open door. "There's the bathroom." He stopped at the end of the hall and opened the shut door, then leaned against the door frame. "And here's where I sleep."

Raina peeked in the door.

Slade snapped his fingers and a dozen candles scattered on the nightstands and dresser burst to life, their flames dancing. They illuminated a room with a king bed decked out in a loud, colorful comforter and black satin sheets.

"Nifty trick."

"That's nothing." He ran an assessing gaze over her, making her catch her breath. "You look like you could use something comfortable to sleep in." It was true. All her things had been left behind in the trunk of her car when they'd transported. She didn't have a toothbrush with her, let alone a change of clothes.

He snapped his fingers. A cool rush of air against her skin prompted her to look down. He'd somehow traded her uniform for a soft, worn hunter-green man's T-shirt that skimmed around her thighs and barely covered her rear. "What, no silk teddy?"

He chuckled. "Don't tempt me. I was trying to be a gentleman. I figured this would be more comfortable. I know you're tired." He moved his fingers, and the rustle of the comforter made her tear her gaze away from him to see the covers being pulled down for her by invisible fingers.

"Now I know you're showing off," she said, her voice laced with sultry amusement.

His lips twitched. "Just a little. Am I scoring any points?"

Raina pulled the elastic band from her hair, letting it uncoil from the tight bun down her back. She ran her fingers over her scalp, letting them slip through her hair, fluffing it. She dipped her chin slightly, lowered her lashes and cast him a sultry look.

"What do you think?"

The color of Slade's eyes lightened several degrees. His pupils grew larger, like a predator scenting its prey. The air between them seemed to swirl with the aroma of leather and cedar. It reminded her of the summers of her youth, carefree and adventurous.

"I think if we let this go any further, you're not going to sleep at all. Get in the bed."

"Are you turning me down, Donovan?"

He took a strand of her hair and rubbed it between his fingers, giving her a half smile. "Absolutely not. Just making sure you're rested enough to enjoy the full experience."

Raina shook her head, strolled past him and climbed between the cool, slick sheets. "You aren't everything you seem, Donovan."

He winked at her. "Neither are you." He snapped his fingers and the candles all went out at once, leaving his large body silhouetted by the light in the hallway. "Sweet dreams."

Slade went out the door, shutting it behind him, then fluxed and phased right back through it. From the shadows he watched her toss and turn until she curled up on her side and her breathing grew slow and regular.

Confident she was sleeping deeply, he phased back through the wall and into the living room, fluxing back to normal. He kicked back in the recliner and flipped on the big-screen television. He left it muted so as not to disturb her. Not that it mattered. He wasn't even aware of what was on the screen. The image of Raina asleep in the bed in the next room kept popping up in his mind, taunting him.

She looked good, fantastic, really, in his bed. Her dusky skin almost glowed when surrounded by the dark sheets, and her dark hair was indistinguishable from the black silk of the pillowcase. Her hair was certainly soft enough to be silk when he'd touched it, as was her bare skin. He'd already bent the rules by glamouring then feeding from her. He'd gone as far as he dared, treading a fine line that, once crossed, couldn't be undone. He didn't dare compound his screwups by indulging himself physically. Nothing good could come from it. Not for him. Definitely not for her.

The problem was his attraction to her wasn't just physical anymore. When she wasn't busy being a nosy cop, Raina actually could let loose and was smart-mouthed enough to keep up with him. She wasn't afraid to get messy or smart off. And she clearly loved motorcycles. All combined into one sexy package that made her very dangerous for him. He'd never let another person get close to the protective armor he'd built around his heart, let alone get past it.

Slade phased himself a beer. He needed a drink. Something stronger than beer would be required to get rid of the ache throbbing against his belly. He tossed the bottle up into the air where it disappeared. The skill of materializing objects had been one of the first things he'd worked to master when he'd become a vampire. Being able to call what he wanted, when he wanted it, meant he'd never be hungry or cold again, huge pluses when you'd lived on the streets. The problem was that didn't cover all the bases.

Sure, being a full vampire was everything he'd expected it to be and more. He'd worked hard to achieve it. But it wasn't everything. Not now.

Deep down there was still a gap that no amount of super skills, excitement, danger or fast motorcycles could fill. A hole that had to do with belonging, not just to a group or a family, but to someone. And somehow Raina had enlarged that hole, making him more aware of it than ever.

Somehow, she'd managed to find her way past his carefully constructed barriers. He was a lot more like Raina than he ever would have guessed. Neither of them were wholly a part of the world in which they lived, and yet each of them had been called upon to be the go-between for their people and the Weres.

"Aren't you going to sleep, too?" Her sleepy voice startled him from his brooding, but the sight of her drained every lucid thought out of his mind.

A cloud of mussed, dark hair hung loose over her shoulders, the long ends of it curling around the subtle curves of her breasts outlined by his T-shirt. Clearly she'd taken off her bra. He liked her wearing his shirt. More, he liked the way it skimmed the tops of her thighs, giving him a peek of the sleek, smooth curve of her ass.

Damn. He looked away and fisted his hand. Being noble sucked. Bad. "You don't need to worry about me. I can go without sleep for days."

She crossed her arms, creating a shelf just under her breasts. "Look, I'm not the only one who needs some sleep. You got beat up far worse than I did the last time we encountered the Weres. That had to take something out of you."

Slade grumbled. She was driving him nuts. For once he was trying to do the right thing rather than find a way to skirt around the rule book. And here she was—temptation at its finest—daring him to step over the line.

Maybe he just needed to clarify the differences between them and show her exactly how real a vampire he was. Scare her off a little. Maybe that would defuse the tension that eddied in the air between them like heat waves off hot asphalt. "Fine. You want to see where I really sleep?"

Her brow furrowed slightly. "I've been sleeping in your bed."

He unfolded himself from the recliner and stalked past her down the hall. Slade ran his hand along the bedroom wall until his fingers encountered the light switch and the switch beside it. He flipped both of them at once.

The room blazed with light and the whole bed began to lift, folding into the wall like a Murphy bed. Beneath it was a king-size hole cut into the bedrock, lined with the same black satin sheets that had been on the bed. He nodded to the hole in the ground. "That's where I *really* sleep."

He watched a shiver skate over her skin and heard her heartbeat pick up the tempo. It looked like a satin-lined grave, and he knew it. That's why he never showed it to anyone who wasn't already vampire.

"You sleep in the ground?"

He leaned his shoulder on the door frame. "Disappointed it wasn't a coffin?"

"No, just wondering why you have a bed if you don't sleep in it."

Slade bent his head and blew out a breath, fighting for control. *Ah, hell. Who was he kidding?* There was only so far he could go with self-denial and she'd just given the final kick to the door of his self-restraint. He'd sampled the smooth texture of her skin, tasted it, sunk his fangs into her and was damn tempted to taste the rest of her, too.

He gazed at her. There was no way he could resist her freshly-tumbled-out-of-bed look and the strawberry-tinted scent of female heat that swirled around her. He wasn't a saint. He was a vampire.

His eyebrow arched up and his lips tilted into a seductive tilt of his mouth that made her stomach swoop. "Would you like me to show you?"

The low, rumbling quality of his voice impacted her like a ride on a throaty motorcycle, making her thighs shake. There was no room for misinterpreting his offer. Raina's skin tightened with expectation. She let her gaze travel from his sculpted mouth made for sinful kisses, to the distracting divot on his chin, then down his chest and lower to the bulge beside the zipper of his pants.

Raina reached down and grazed her hand over his hardened length. "I can think of something I'd like to see a whole lot more."

He groaned, closing his eyes for a moment, tipping his head back, and when he opened them and stared down at her they were the color of caramel, dark with desire. *Flick*. His fangs extended fully, indenting his bottom lip. "Not pulling any punches, are you?" The edge of his voice was raspy with barely leashed control.

Raina looked up at him through the fan of her lashes, and the tip of her tongue traced a slow, slick path over her top lip. His pupils dilated. His eager response made her giddy with power. Her pulse spread out to her fingertips, then traveled lower to the apex of her thighs.

A sensual smile curved her lips. "Why should I? There's no crime in knowing exactly what you want." She grabbed handfuls of his shirt and pulled him into her, kissing him fiercely. Letting all the pent-up desire she'd been shutting away out into the open. His kiss, hot, firm and demanding, caused the slow burn inside her to flare into full flame. She wrapped her arms around his neck, holding on as the need took her in a heated wave.

Determined to bring him as close to the edge as she was, she deliberately laved the length of first one fang in a slow sensual slide of her tongue and then the other, knowing it would arouse him further.

Slade growled, the sound vibrating against her mouth and shimmering down her body as he wrapped his strong arms around her and lifted her off the floor, crushing her against his chest. His kisses, powerful, raw and needy, stripped away her ability to breathe and made her squirm. Heat pooled low in her belly, making her thighs slick. She wanted him. All of him.

"You're dangerous. You know that?" he murmured between drugging kisses as he flipped the switch on the wall and stalked toward the descending bed and tossed her onto it. She bounced slightly on the mattress. Raina propped herself up on her elbows and then crooked her finger in a come-here motion.

Slade's jaw jumped and tensed as he grasped the edge of his T-shirt and peeled it off over his head in one fluid movement, tossing it to the floor. He was gorgeous. The broad span of his shoulders and his powerfully built torso and arms made her pulse with need. It had been so long since she'd let herself go that all her senses were hyperaware of him. The dark storm raging behind his eyes, the leather scent that mixed with the smell of clean male, the touch of his hands on her.

Raina lifted her leg and with her foot she stroked the hard curve of his pecs and down the ridges of his abdomen, following the dark trail of hair that disappeared beneath the waistband of his pants. With her toes she tugged at the edge of his waistband. "Pants, too."

"Vixen," Slade murmured as he shucked off his pants. Raina made a low sound deep in her throat at the sight of him bold and aroused. She'd suspected that he was built, but not nearly as well as this. She sat up and circled his penis with her hand, lightly stroking the silken hot length of it and brushing the small bead of moisture at the tip with the pad of her thumb.

Slade closed his eyes and fisted his hands by his sides, letting her do whatever she pleased, which only made her more brazen. Raina traced the same path of her thumb with her tongue, surprised at the smoothness of his skin, then slid her mouth over him.

He shuddered. "Are you trying to kill me?"

She released him and gave a throaty laugh. "Where would the fun be in that?" She patted the bed beside her. He sank down, stretching out on the mattress. The hot, hard length of his body beside hers warmed her, but it wasn't nearly enough.

Raina twisted in one smooth move, straddling him.

His erection pulsed against her, but was blocked by damp underwear. "But first, I think you need to show me a few of your vampire skills. If you're so good at phasing things, could you take care of—"

Faster than she could blink, he phased away both her T-shirt and her underwear, leaving her deliciously naked and suddenly intimately pressed against him. The brush of air caused her skin to contract, making it even more sensitive. Raina gasped at the sensation and lightly grazed her wet heat against the length of his shaft, teasing both him and herself. "Nice. Very nice."

Slade grasped her hips, his large hands partially cupping her bottom on each side. His eyes were luminous, glittering with need. "Now I know you're trying to kill me," he muttered, as he flexed against her wet heat and kissed her deeply.

She placed her hands on his muscled shoulders and lifted up, the air space between them leaving her wanting more of him. Raina broke their kiss, staring down at him, both of them surrounded by a curtain of her dark hair. "Are you going to touch me, or do I need to draw you a diagram?" she teased.

Her challenge apparently hit home. His expression changed from restrained heat to intense raw sexuality in a heartbeat as he grasped her by the hips and rolled them over.

"How about you tell me when I find it?" His mouth slanted hot and hard over hers as his hand slipped around the curve of her buttock, squeezing her bare bottom.

She broke their kiss. "Lower," she urged.

His deft fingers moved down along the seam of her buttocks, then threaded through her curls and skimmed along her damp folds, stroking her as he kissed a searing path across her breasts and down her ribs. Raina bucked as the tension inside her coiled even tighter.

He raised his mouth from her skin. "Am I getting warm?" he chuckled.

"Deeper."

He scraped his fangs along the ridge of her hip, sending small tremors shooting along every nerve ending. Raina gasped as he slipped a finger inside and slid his thumb over the small nub hidden within her cleft, then moved both in unison. She lifted into the sensation, her breath shallow and fast as sparks ignited under her skin, turning to starbursts before her eyes.

"What about now?"

"More!" she moaned.

Slade felt her shake beneath his hands as he withdrew his fingers and cupped her bottom, lifting her. He lightly scraped a path along the smooth, sleek skin of her inner thigh, laving the abraded skin as he came closer to her damp, fragrant heat, enjoying the sound she made. He'd known she would be hot, but never this responsive.

He swirled a path with his tongue where his fingers had been repaying her the torment she'd given him. Raina writhed, fisting her hands in the silk sheets. Slade suckled her hard, pulling from her the last bits of her control and resistance. Raina arched, a moan sliding from her throat as her body convulsed.

Not satisfied to merely torment her, Slade slipped his fingers into the slick smoothness of her, setting a rhythm that had Raina panting and writhing against his touch. He wanted to watch her come undone. Her skin shimmered with perspiration, her heartbeat pounding so fast and hard that it sounded like a heavy driving bass guitar.

"Am I getting warmer?" he asked, his tone seductive and low as he moved over her, their sweat-slickened skin causing him to slide over her curves.

Her dark eyes glittered, a bit manic. "Red-hot, but what I want is to feel you." She ran her hand along the smooth, hard planes of his back and over his hip, sliding her hand between them and grasping him in her hand.

Slade bucked, almost losing it. Damn, he loved that she knew what she wanted. She lifted her hips, drawing him into her silken heat. He sank home. The effect was electric, rocketing through him with a jolt that left him stunned. Her body, inside and out, tightened, going rigid. Slade cried out and Raina joined him, her heart beating hard enough against his chest that he could have sworn it beat for both of them.

He touched his forehead to hers, brushing kisses over her cheeks and along her mouth. "You okay?" He was terrified that in his need to have her he'd gone too far and hurt her.

"I'm…better…than…okay," she said breathlessly. "I just can't move."

Slade chuckled. "Let me take care of that." He curved his arm around her and rolled slowly, clasping her soft, sleek body to him until she rested against his chest. Her hot, moist skin and supple body were limp and relaxed against him. He gently brushed aside the dark strands of hair sticking to her damp cheek, then ran his fingers down her back in a smooth, gliding touch that followed her spine.

"Mmm. That's nice," she murmured against his skin, her voice sleepy. He drew the sheets and blankets up around them then continued to stroke small circles on her skin until her breathing changed, becoming slow and rhythmic.

Somehow, she'd stopped the crazy world and for a moment there was peace. The tranquility of the moment hit him hard. How long had it been since he'd felt this way? Never.

She snuggled up closer and he wrapped her in his arms. He relaxed into the moment, letting it fill him up, knowing that he'd need it…later.

The wolves ran through his dreams, snapping and howling, their eyes reflecting the orange-red flicker of the campfire, making them look like hellhounds. They circled, closing ranks, and yipping to one another as they came together, shoulder to shoulder.

Just beyond the rim of the fire's light were the shadowy figures of humans standing in an outer circle. Voices joined in a slow, rhythmic chant measured by a drum, echoing like a second heartbeat in his ears. He tried to crawl away from the center of the circle only to find himself nose to snarling muzzle with one of the wolves.

The chanting pounded in his brain, *jus-tice, jus-tice,*

jus-tice, and he dug his fingernails into his scalp, ripping downward across his ears trying to make it stop.

The drums and chanting stopped.

The wolves advanced.

He screamed as one gripped him by the throat and
the others sank in their teeth and tore him apart.

Only suddenly he wasn't the one in the circle any
longer. He was alone, looking through the trees at his
mother, her slender hand raised and shaking as bits of
her clothing and hair flew outward, her screams piercing his ears. A wolf turned, stared at him, his muzzle
red with gore, the flesh and blood of his mother. Slade
huddled closer to the tree, wishing he could simply disappear.

Something soft stroked the side of his face and his
eyes snapped open. He inhaled deeply and found his
nose filled with the sweet, womanly scent of Raina.
The aching muscles in his back and stomach released.

"You were having a bad dream," she whispered. "A
pretty violent one from the look of it."

With aching realization, his chest grew heavy. He
tossed the tangled sheets aside, letting the night air cool
his skin. "It wasn't a daymare. It was a memory." He
turned, pulling her close to him. "I remember what happened to my mother. I was there."

Raina gasped, her fingers covering the open O of
her mouth, her hand shaking. "You couldn't have been
more than seven or eight years old," she whispered, her
voice husky with emotion.

"I was eight. Those wolves that killed my mother—"

he looked deeply into her eyes "—are part of the Wenatchee Were pack, right?"

Raina bit her lip and nodded. "They said she'd betrayed the alpha. She was to be his mate. She'd stolen Bracken's child away from them."

This time his eyes widened. "You were there?"

Raina squeezed her eyes shut, trying to block out the bitter memory and shuddered. "It's part of the reason I never wanted to be the Whisperer. I saw what the ancestors did to her when I was just six. How can they call that justice? She didn't ask to be part of their stupid pack. She was chosen, without her consent, just like me. They were the ancestors. They were supposed to take care of us. I had no idea they were shifters."

Slade pulled her into his bare chest, holding her close. "I'm not going to let anything happen to you. I swear it." For the moment Raina let herself take comfort in his strong arms, but deep down she knew it wouldn't last.

"What are we going to do?"

Slade glanced at the clock. "Well, we've slept the day away. It's about time we head down to Sangria and see what we can dig up from the others to help us with our plan."

Chapter 13

Evening traffic streaked by on the street, the headlights bobbing as Slade and Raina cruised by on the downtown streets of Seattle. Music, a combination of guitar and drums and enthusiastic singing, drifted up from the waterfront on the evening breeze coming off the Puget Sound. Overhead, the red throbbing beat of the neon Sangria sign over the club door reminded Raina of a heartbeat.

"So if this is where the Cascade Clan hangs out topside, why isn't there something like it in the clan complex?"

Slade glanced at her. "Because not everyone who comes here is a vampire. Some are donors and others are just normal mortals out for an evening. This is just the place where all those worlds collide."

"And what about the Weres? If they come out do you think they'll ever be welcome here?"

Slade snorted. "Not likely. Do you have any idea how many brawls they'd start?" He opened the padded black leather-studded door for her.

Inside, Sangria looked like a combination trendy popular dance club and an underground cavern with up-lit stalactites and down-lit stalagmites conspicuously placed to bracket the cushy crimson velvet booths. The booths, which lined the right wall, edged the pale wood dance floor that pulsated with a light show and a noisy crowd.

Raina focused past the driving bass of the music and moving bodies, concentrating instead on taking in her surroundings—looking for exits and determining any potential problems. To the left was a long, highly polished black-and-chrome bar with mirror-backed shelves filled with various bottles. To the back were a series of velvet curtains. "So what's behind the curtains?"

Slade arched a brow. "Ignore what's behind the curtain."

"So said the Wizard of Oz." She snickered. "Seriously, what's back there? Gambling? Illegal activity?"

"Always thinking like a cop, aren't you?"

Raina lifted her chin. "Suspicion and observation comes with the territory, kind of like having to drink blood if you're a vampire."

"They're the tasting rooms for the club. Rare vintage wines, blood, absinthe. Whatever legally turns on the patrons."

"Does the clan run this club?"

Slade nodded. "In fact, see that big dark-headed guy over there? He runs it. That's Dmitri Dionotte, our clan *Trejan.*"

Standing with his big hands on the shoulders of a blonde, Dmitri seemed almost as imposing and intense as Achilles, but far darker and more serious, like Slade. She recognized Dr. Chamberlin seated beside the blonde and Achilles next to her.

"What's a *Trejan?*"

"Our version of a vice president. He's second in command and Achilles reports to him. If we're going to hit the Weres, the order will have to come down from Dmitri." Slade grabbed hold of her hand, steering her through the crowded club toward their table.

"Is that why we're really here? To feel out if we can get permission to trap a Were and bring him back for questioning?"

Slade smiled at her, the tips of his fangs showing. "Bingo, babe. Now you're thinking like a security operative."

Raina noted the slight tone of pride in his voice and was pleasantly surprised at the warmth spreading through her chest at his approval. Since when she did care what Slade thought of her? Her lips tingled at the thought of their first kiss in the tent. She found herself touching her lips and forced herself to lower her hand.

Slade pulled up beside their table. "*Trejan,* Achilles, ladies," he said as he inclined his head.

"Evening, Donovan," Dmitri responded. He shifted his dark gaze to her and Raina felt it melt all the way through her like a laser beam. "Is this Officer Raven-wing?"

Raina swallowed the bubble of discomfort that had lodged in her throat and moved to shake hands with Dmitri. It wouldn't do to look like a coward in front of vampires who were clearly in charge of things. "Nice to meet you."

"Achilles tells me you have the dubious honor of being a Wolf Whisperer." All curious gazes around the table turned to her. The combination of having so many vampires so intently focused on her caused her stomach to swish. Raina fleetingly hoped the floor would open up and swallow her whole.

"That's amazing," commented the blonde, filling the awkward silence that stretched among all of them. "Since my husband can't seem to introduce me, I'm Kristin." She held out a hand to Raina and gave her a warm smile, which accented her sparkling blue eyes.

Slade leaned in close and whispered in a conspiratorial nature in Raina's ear. "She's a reporter."

"Must you tell everyone that before I even can find out something about them?" Kristin sighed. "My interviewing skills are going to get rusty if you keep that up." She turned her attention back to Raina. "So what's a Wolf Whisperer?"

"I always thought it was an honorary tribal title, but apparently it means I can talk to the shifters," she said with a lightness she was far from feeling. Being in the heart of vampireville topside caused her senses to go into overdrive and she was nearly getting eyestrain from trying to be constantly vigilant.

"Surely they can speak just fine when they are in their mortal forms?" Dr. Chamberlin asked.

"No, she can talk to them when they are wolves," Slade explained.

Kristin's eyes glittered with avid interest. She rested her chin on the heel of her hand. "Really? How did you find out you could do that?"

"Well, I—" Raina sensed Slade's tension increase just a second before he cut her off. He didn't want her saying anything to the others. Why? Was he that afraid of what might happen if he happened to transition?

"*Trejan,* we'd like approval to bring a Were back for questioning."

Dmitri and Achilles glanced at each other then back at Slade. "Achilles has told me about your report. But in assessing the situation we both feel you going back into Were territory this close to the full moon would be an unacceptable risk."

"What you mean is you don't trust me and Ravenwing to swing it without getting caught by the Weres."

Achilles squeezed one hand closed, using his thumb to crack his knuckles one by one. "I know you aren't questioning your *Trejan's* direct order, are you?" The threatening tone in his voice left no room for doubt that their idea of using Raina as bait to go into the shifter territory had fallen flat.

"What about Raina?" Slade pushed. "She's probably the best chance we have of getting a Were to come close without causing an all-out confrontation."

Achilles shifted his gaze to Raina. "As a Whisperer, you know that the shifters have a claim on you, don't you? They'd be well within their rights to kill any vampire holding you back from them."

Raina crossed her arms. "Last time I checked, I had a say in the matter, same as Kaycee did."

A meaningful glance passed between Achilles and Dmitri. "Are you aware of what happens to Whisperers who don't follow the directions of the Weres' alpha?" Dmitri asked.

Raina's face tightened and heated. "Yes. Very aware."

Achilles shook his head. "It's a big risk. Too big."

"Isn't that my call?" Raina said.

Slade grabbed hold of her hand and gave it a reassuring squeeze.

Dmitri shifted his stance. "Are you willing to have another vampire accompany you besides Donovan?"

Raina pushed her chin out a little farther, and tried to stand taller, not that she and Dmitri would ever see eye to eye, he was so much taller than she was. "No. I'll go on my own."

"Absolutely not." Achilles stood up abruptly. "You wouldn't stand a chance."

"A few large animal tranqs and a night scope and I think I'd do just fine. It's not as if I've never gone up against big game before in my job." Visions of the pissed-off mama bear trying to untree her cub out of a maple in the front yard of Janice Taylor's house rose to mind. Sure, she'd been able to subdue the bear, but moving her had taken four officers and three other people from animal control. "The only thing I might need is help bringing him back here."

"You sound very determined," Dmitri said, his lips tipping up at the corner. "Sounds like someone else I know." He glanced affectionately down at his wife.

"If she wants Slade to go with her, I say we let him," Dr. Chamberlin said. "We're less than a week out from the full moon and I think I've developed something that could mitigate his symptoms."

"But his moon sickness is getting worse. He could transition out there, and then where would Officer Ravenwing be?" Achilles countered.

"Left to use her skills as a Wolf Whisperer," Kristin cut in. "Look, if she can talk to the Weres, then even if Slade transitions they can still communicate. Just because he might transition isn't a reason for him to avoid this assignment altogether."

"Thank you," Slade said, with a nod in Kristin's direction.

Dmitri huffed. "You're interfering in clan security matters again, wife."

Kristin threw him an arch smile. "And your point would be?"

Dmitri rolled his eyes. Dr. Chamberlin chuckled. Raina tried to take it all in as they talked among one another, squabbling and laughing, all working together. The dynamics of the clan were far different than she'd imagined they'd be. This was more like a large extended family than simply a society.

They ordered drinks for everyone and she picked a shot of whiskey, while Slade ordered a beer. The flow of conversation and the warm air in the club lulled her into a relaxed state. But the memory of Kaycee's brutal death made a full-body shiver ripple over her. She tried to picture Slade as the young boy alone, without a memory of who he was, and her heart twisted uncomfortably. Raina took a sip of her whiskey and let the liquid slide down her throat in a slow burn.

She couldn't imagine her life without the tribe she'd grown up in. The annual customs had set her routine, the tribal meetings more like extended family parties. Her mother and father had always maintained a calm, steady influence on her life. They were strict but kind. Without all of them she'd be rootless, ungrounded and blown about by the winds of life.

Clearly Slade had found a similar place where he belonged among these vampires. And that place was in now in jeopardy. Raina decided then and there that she'd do what she could to help him resolve this and protect his place among his people.

She could certainly understand Achilles's concerns. If Slade did transition out there, she'd need to be able to act quickly. While Slade might be able to fight off a group of Weres with his vampire skills, she'd be left with just her wits, her weapons and her tranq darts.

"Does anyone know what happens once a Were transitions?" she asked as she tapped her finger thoughtfully against her glass. The flow of conversation around the table stopped dead. "I mean, can't they move back and forth between the two forms? Wouldn't he be able to choose what form he was in, even if it does happen out there?" She looked hopefully at Dr. Chamberlin.

The doctor shrugged as she picked up her glass of

red wine and took a sip. At least Raina thought it was red wine; she didn't want to examine it too closely.

"Honestly, we don't know. Everything I've been able to dig up on it says that around the full moon the shifting stabilizes into the lycan form. They can't shift back to their human form until the moon begins to wane again."

Raina estimated that left them about three days. That was cutting things close if they wanted to capture Ty, interrogate him and make plans to resist whatever plans the Were pack had rolling.

"But considering Slade isn't fully Were, wouldn't that change things? Wouldn't he potentially have more control?" Raina asked.

Achilles leaned in, putting his elbows on the table. "That's the problem—nobody knows. This isn't something that normally happens. Traditionally, we vampires and the Weres have maintained our territorial boundaries. We don't mix with them and they don't mix with us. I didn't think a vampire of Donovan's stripe was even possible. No offense, Donovan."

"None taken," Slade said, tipping his bottle of beer in Achilles's direction.

The first heated rush of anger had begun to abate, leaving a gaping hole that hurt far worse. While the doc and Kristen were newcomers to the clan, Slade had vivid recollections of the others from his childhood. Achilles and Dmitri hadn't changed at all. No. That wasn't true. While they looked just the same as they always had, there had been changes. Both of them had found mates and seemed far happier, even though the challenges of the past year had been intense.

The thought of being cast out of the clan made him physically ill. Worse than moon sickness did. And the beer wasn't settling his stomach. Everything he knew, everything he'd worked for, was tied up in this clan. If he didn't have them, he'd have nothing—be nothing—all over again. He began picking at the label on his beer bottle, peeling it off in strips. Thoughts, fears and worries rolled around in his head, smacking against each other like the balls on a pool table after a clean break.

He shifted forward in his chair, catching both Dmitri's and Achilles's gazes. "So do we have your permission to tag us a Were and bring him back?" he asked, keeping his voice even, and ruthlessly keeping hidden even a hint of his inner turmoil.

Achilles looked to Dmitri and Dmitri nodded. "There's just one thing, Donovan. Make this operation clean. I don't want any loose ends or hurt mortals," he said as he glanced in Raina's direction.

Slade nodded and relaxed back in his chair. Good. Now they were getting somewhere.

"I've got a serum I'd like to administer to you before you leave," Dr. Chamberlin added.

"No problemo," Slade said. He looked over at Raina. "Those shifters won't even know what hit them."

Dmitri gave a mirthless laugh. "That's not the only hit they're unprepared for. The shifters don't know what they're asking for when it comes to introducing themselves to mortal society," he said as he leaned back in his chair, his arm resting around the Kristin's back.

"What do you mean?" Raina asked.

"Think about it," Kristin said. "In a world that values digital entertainment and artificial cooling, light and heating even more than land and water, do you really think the Weres are going to be able to hold their own?"

Raina shrugged. "They're stronger than humans and they've lasted this long."

"Yeah, but the mortals outnumber them," Slade said. "This isn't the old days where they could control a tribe who had a parallel belief system and revered them and nature. This is the twenty-first century. If they push at the mortals to get control over a larger territory, they're going to get their asses handed to them with a side of silver."

"And why do you care? I thought vampires hated Weres."

"We don't hate them. We just don't respect them," Achilles said matter-of-factly. "They're like animals, only concerned with their own needs."

"So if you think that wandering into your territory isn't going work out well for them, how would it impact your clan?"

"If they rile up the mortals, you can bet vampires are going to catch it, too," Dmitri said, his dark brows drawing together. "Our clan has a fragile peace going with the locals. We don't need some testosterone-filled bunch of hair balls lousing it up by coming in here and ripping apart some mortals to prove a useless point."

"Out in the wild, what happens when one wolf pack invades another's territory?" Dr. Chamberlin asked.

Raina tucked her hair behind her ear. "They get frenzied, trying to compete with one another to claim food. But the Weres don't feed on people like vampires do, do they?"

"No, but Eris does," Achilles muttered. "She feeds on their misery, anger, pain and suffering, and if she can, she'll get the Weres to cause as much chaos as possible."

"Which means…" Raina said slowly, her gaze going from one somber-looking vampire to the next.

Slade's heated gaze connected with hers. "Which means, babe, unless you and I pull this off, we're screwed."

Chapter 14

The plan had seemed incredibly simple when they'd drawn it out on paper. Slade would flux invisible. They'd creep to the Weres' back door, then she'd reach out to them, calling them to her. Once she made contact, if it wasn't Ty that came for her, she'd ask to speak to him. Then Slade could slip a silver chain over him and they'd transport back to the clan, Were in tow.

Easy, clean, simple. But now that she was sitting at the stream that marked the edge of the shifter's territory, she wasn't so sure. Wind whispered through the woods, making dried leaves rattle and goose bumps pimple her skin. Evening shadows gathered and stretched over the landscape with tenacious dark fingers.

She rubbed her arms trying to ward off the sudden

chill invading her bones. "Do you really think this is going to work?"

"Babe, you reek of Were-bait," he whispered low enough for only her to hear.

"Fabulous," she said without enthusiasm.

"Trust me, they won't be able to resist you."

Raina controlled the urge to reach out and touch him. It was disconcerting talking to Slade when he was invisible. She felt as though she were talking to an imaginary friend. For a second Raina wondered what other powers vampires possessed. If they could read minds, and go invisible, did they also have X-ray vision?

"Shouldn't you be somewhere else so they can't smell you out?" she asked, her voice barely above a whisper. She didn't know if Weres had the same super-hearing vampires appeared to.

"We're downwind. They won't know what hit 'em until they're laid out flat."

Raina stared down into the shifting waters of the creek as it swirled golden aspen leaves around the smooth stones. Slade's grazing touch on her shoulder made her start.

"Be careful but don't be scared," he whispered in her ear, the words warm against the skin of her nape, sending a delicious shiver down her skin. "I'll be right with you the whole time."

Raina took a shaky, deep breath. She closed her eyes, trying to center herself, then cupped her hands around her mouth and called out as loudly as she could. The series of howls and yips she let out were responded to almost instantly by a howling chorus in return.

Minutes later the large wolves melted through the trees, seeming to appear out of thin air from behind the massive trunks. She recognized Ty by the darker ruff of fur, like a dark gray collar, about his throat.

"I've come to speak to you, brothers," she called out.

Ty sniffed the air, his keen gaze darting about the clearing. "Where is your vampire?"

Raina snorted. "He's not *my* vampire."

"Why do you come to us?"

She glanced at the four other wolves, two flanking each side of Ty. "I have news from across the mountain. But I would only speak with your leader."

Ty stalked toward her slowly, circling her, his warm breath huffing at her clothing. He sniffed the air, his furry brows bending over deep brown eyes. "Take her to Bracken," he ordered.

Raina turned, looking at the large wolf beside her. "No! Wait, I meant I wanted to talk to you."

The wolf's mouth elongated into somewhere between a smile and a snarl, his black lips pulled tight over his pointed teeth. "I know what you meant, Whisperer. But in this pack we all follow Bracken's lead. He, and no other, will decide what is to be done with you."

Slade cursed silently to himself as he watched the four escorts close in around Raina, one in front, one behind, and two on either side of her. He didn't want to endanger her by taking out the wolves with her in the center but Dmitri had been specific. No casualties.

He calculated the possibilities. He could perhaps take out two of them before the other three knew what was happening, but there was no way he could take out four without Ty becoming aware of his presence.

Raina's hiking boots splashed in the creek as they crossed the water. She glanced back in Slade's direction, even though he was invisible.

"Your vampire can follow along if he is brave enough to," Ty said, his tone mocking. "And if your vampire is fool enough to leave you to us, we'll use you as bait to lure him out. Duamish still wants blood payment for his brother. And he doesn't care if he takes it from the vampire or from you."

Damn. There wasn't much choice. If they took her to Bracken there'd be far more shifters to deal with than just five. Slade released his flux, turning visible once more. "You made your point. Let her go."

Ty turned, his tail twitching, the hair forming a bristled edge along his back. "What makes you think we won't just take you, too?"

Slade gave a harsh bark of laughter. "Because you couldn't do it the first time you tried. And the odds aren't any better. Besides, this is a diplomatic mission. We're just here to get some answers."

"You're trespassing."

"Didn't think you'd reply to an engraved invitation to meet."

Ty bent his head, hunching his shoulders. Slade knew from the last time he was shifting into his human form. "You might want to shut your eyes for a moment, Raina," he called out.

She trusted him enough to do as he told her, but

the wet pop and crunch as Ty shifted forms made her flinch. "What's going on?" she asked.

"I've shifted into my human form," Ty answered.

Raina opened her eyes, gasped and shut them again, a blush coloring her skin. Ty chuckled. "Obviously she's yet to see what a real man looks like, vampire."

The insult was obvious, but Slade had bigger matters on his mind than meaningless posturing. "This meeting is just between us. Tell the pups to go home."

Ty's shoulder and chest muscles flexed, and he gritted his teeth. He locked gazes with Slade, the tension stretching out between them. For a moment Slade thought he'd do just the opposite and order an attack, but Ty barked at his followers to return to their den. They slowly moved away, casting uncertain backward glances as they slunk off into the woods, their tails tucked down.

"Is it safe for me to look yet?" Raina asked.

Slade phased a pair of jeans onto Ty, who glared at him and growled in response. "If I wanted to wear clothes, vampire, I'm perfectly capable of doing so myself."

"This isn't for you, it's for the lady," Slade shot back. "Good to go, Raina."

She cracked open one eye and then the other, then turned around in a small circle on the spot as if she were still expecting the wolves to be surrounding her. "Where'd they all go?"

Neither of the men answered her, their gazes locked on one another.

"You got what you wanted, vampire. Ask your questions and get out of our territory."

"Not yet."

Still focused on the Were, he nodded once and Raina let a loop of thin silver chain fly lassolike around Ty's chest, binding his arms to his sides. He growled and gnashed his teeth, straining against the metal bonds. "What are you doing?"

"Just a little insurance policy to make sure you cooperate. Silver is just as disruptive to you as it is to me, so your Whisperer is the only one here who can remove it without being harmed."

Under the influence of the silver Ty began to sway slightly, falling to one knee. He cursed. Apparently the silver was far more potent on Weres than vampires, but she had no way to be sure. She'd never seen a vampire bound by silver. Hell, until this last week she hadn't even realized her own ancestor spirits were werewolves.

Raina moved quickly, bending down on one knee to get eye to eye with the shifter. Slade had briefed her on the specific questions they needed answers to most. They both figured Ty would answer her before he'd answer Slade. "Is Bracken in league with Eris?"

Ty lifted his brown eyes, now glassy with pain, to stare at her. A pang of guilt tugged at her gut. He'd cooperated with them fully and was now suffering for it. Somehow, deep down, part of her felt the vampire's logic was deeply flawed. Part animal or not, the Weres, like the vampires, were basically human at the core. Cords of muscle stood out along either side of Ty's neck as he struggled against the toxicity of the silver.

"The goddess calls down the moon and we must listen." He groaned.

Slade stepped forward. "Calls down the moon, what the h—"

Raina held up a hand, stopping Slade. "What's her plan?"

Ty hung his head, shaking it back and forth, his heavy dark hair swinging with the motion. "The goddess commands us to take the vampire territory. To subdue them. They have risen up against her. They must be made to respect her."

Raina's gaze connected with Slade's. It was obvious to her that the Were was fading fast. "Does Bracken know who Kaycee's child is?"

That got a reaction. Ty snapped his head up, his eyes narrowing in fierce concentration. "The last Whisperer was Bracken's mate. The child was his. She betrayed us all, taking the child with her and going to the bloodsuckers. They contaminated both her and the child." He flicked a disgusted glance in Slade's direction, then turned his attention back to her. Pain shimmered in the depths of his brown eyes.

Slade shifted uncomfortably beside her. Raina could sense his tension. "But did Bracken ever find the child?"

"The elders found Kaycee and brought her back to fulfill her duty. She'd already borne and raised the child among the vampires. He was marked on his heel, bitten by Bracken himself to insure the child would grow to be one of us regardless of his impurity. But after Kaycee was tried by the elders, the child disappeared."

Ty's glassy gaze shifted to Slade as he swayed. "Bracken's given strict orders. If we find his son we should kill him." His eyes rolled to white and the Were passed out, falling over onto the leaf-littered ground.

Raina moved to slip the silver chain off the shifter, but Slade grabbed her hand. "Give it a minute. We need him out long enough to transport him."

"You're not seriously still thinking of taking him back with us?"

"Hell, yeah, I am. Achilles can get specifics out of him. The numbers in the pack. Their strategies. He's one hell of an interrogator. Learned a few tricks back when he was a Spartan that don't exactly fall under the Geneva Convention."

Raina stared hard at him. "You are *not* going to torture him. He cooperated with us. We're the ones who are acting out of line."

"Look, this isn't some card game where fairness counts. They've already tried to kill you once. You heard him, Eris is commanding them to whip the vampires back to her side or wipe them out. You can't expect me to stand by and do nothing. A war is coming."

She shook her head. "I'm not asking you to do nothing, I'm asking you to just stop and think about this. If we take him, and he's harmed, then any chance we have at a diplomatic solution is screwed."

Slade's jaw worked back and forth. "Achilles knows

what he's doing, and I have my orders. We're bringing the shifter in."

With that Slade hefted Ty like a sack of grain over one shoulder, grabbed her about the waist and transported them back to Seattle.

They arrived in the security room in a swirl of dark particles. Other than the humming computers, no one was on duty. Raina had trouble regaining her balance and leaned against the long conference table at the center of the room for support. She wasn't sure if she'd ever get used to Slade's unusual means of transportation.

"So now what?" she asked, perching herself on the edge of the desk while Slade propped an unconscious Ty up in a chair. "You can't just drop him off, and you can't truss him up with silver. It might kill him."

"It did seem to weaken him a hell of a lot faster than it does a vampire."

"Maybe their chemistry is different, just like their virus being more virulent that the vampire strain."

Slade closed his eyes, ignoring her, and for a moment Raina was peeved by his apparent rudeness. Beside him, a shape formed out of a smokelike substance into Achilles. She realized he must have been calling to Achilles and felt sheepish about her attitude.

Achilles eyed Ty in his human form. "So this is what they look like when they aren't wearing fur, huh?"

"You've never seen them in human form?"

Both vampires turned and stared at her. Slade shrugged. "Why would we? They've never come onto our territory and we've always stayed out of theirs until now."

Achilles laid a hand on Slade's shoulder. "Good work, solider. I'll take things from here. Why don't you return Officer Ravenwing to your quarters where she can get cleaned up and rested while you report to the council."

A flicker of dread crossed Slade's face, but he silently nodded. "Come on, Raina. I'll take you to my apartment."

Raina wasn't going to have any of it. Knowing how the vampires felt about the Weres, she wasn't about to abandon Ty, who was still technically part of her tribe by distant mythical relation, to Achilles without at least some supervision. "You go on ahead. I'm staying here."

Slade cursed under his breath and looked to his commander. "You want me to take her anyway?"

Raina bristled. She might not be a vampire, but she certainly wasn't going to let them tell her what she could and couldn't do and where she would or wouldn't go. "I said, I'm staying here," she said firmly.

Achilles jerked his head at Slade. "Go on, it's not smart to keep the council waiting."

Slade gave her a last glance, filled with a mixture of trepidation and sadness, and then turned from solid muscle and bone to insubstantial black mist and finally vanished altogether.

"So what does the council need to see Slade about? He didn't look too happy."

Achilles kept his focus on Ty as he replied. "Vampire business. And he looks that way because the only time we get called before the clan council is when it's something critical. Otherwise Laird Petrov or Dmitri call the shots." He glanced at her. "How long did you have him chained up?"

"Less than fifteen minutes."

Achilles inspected the dark red, blistered skin that formed a ring around Ty's torso. He shook his head, rubbing his finger over his mouth. "I might need to have the doc take a look at him."

Raina bit back a gasp of surprise. It didn't seem that Achilles planned to hurt Ty at all. "Are you going to question him?"

The large vampire glanced at her. "Yeah. But not until he's conscious and gotten medical care."

"What if he doesn't feel like talking to you?"

Achilles gave her a thousand-watt smile. "Well, since you volunteered to stay behind, I was hoping he'd talk to you instead. I'll just flux and stay here in the room with you two."

"How am I going to know what you want answered?"

Achilles pointed to the laptop behind her on the conference table. "I'll send it to you in text. That way he won't hear me, either."

Slade materialized in front of the enormous, intricately carved black double doors, bracketed on either side by uniformed men all in black—the council's personal guard. Emblazoned on the outside of the doors was the red insignia of the clan, three interlocked circles that formed an inverted triangle, like a fang. Achilles had explained to the Shyelds that the circles stood for life, death and vampire—each interdependent with the other, but none the same.

For a moment, Slade wondered how it would change if the Weres won. With Eris on their side, it was a strong possibility, but one he didn't want to think about too much. His stomach was already an oily mess of fear, anger and worry. The council didn't just call up a vampire for a friendly chat. Whatever was going down was serious.

The doors cracked open, swinging inward, their movement making the light from the ornately scrolled candelabras within the council chamber flicker ominously. Dmitri glanced at Slade and waved him inside.

Slade had only been in the room twice before. Once during his initiation as a full Shyeld and again during his petition for transitioning into a full-blooded vampire.

A crimson velvet curtain lined large portions of the dark rock walls. Nine occupied, carved cherrywood chairs sat in a semicircle around a black-tiled dais with the clan's symbol marked in a contrasting red rock against the surrounding smooth black stone. The largest and grandest of the chairs sat at the center and was occupied by the clan's laird, Roman Petrov. His dark cloak fell about him in folds.

Dmitri stood off to the side of the dais, hands clasped behind him at the center of his back. Slade climbed to the center of the dais, where he'd been twice before and, like Dmitri, he stood at attention, waiting for the laird's words.

Slade sensed Roman's dark eyes peeling him apart, searching for imperfections, but Slade remained impassive, stuffing down the insecure emotions wreaking havoc on his mind.

"It has come to our attention, Mr. Donovan, that you have an unusual condition that makes you a potential danger to our clan."

Slade held his tongue and stared resolutely ahead. Better he didn't say anything than speak out too soon and be out of turn. He knew whatever they were going to tell him had already been deliberated behind closed doors.

"Dr. Chamberlin believes that your condition can be stabilized to render you safe. We have decided to allow you to remain within the protection of our clan, as is your right, unless you happen to transition fully into a shape-shifter. Should that occur, your clearance and your position in this clan would be revoked. We cannot risk that your mixed blood might taint the others in this clan, spreading the shifter's virus within our own clan."

The words hit like a sucker punch to the gut, taking the wind out of him. Slade remained upright and kept from coughing out of sheer willpower and determination—the same things that had kept him alive out on the streets. Mixed blood. So the truth was out. He could just imagine what kind of reaction he'd get from the others once they found out the truth.

"I understand, my laird." Slade said nothing more because there was nothing he could say. It had already been decided, just like Achilles thought it might be. If he turned Were, for any reason, even to save one of the other vampires in battle, he'd be kicked to the curb. He saluted Roman and the rest of the council members respectfully with his fisted hand across his chest and a bowed head, then stepped down of the dais and quickly exited the chamber before his legs went wobbly.

Dmitri's arm around his shoulder stabilized him as the council chamber doors shut behind them. "That went a lot better than I thought it would," Dmitri said.

Slade glanced at him. Right now he just wanted to keep the bile rising up at the back of his throat where it belonged. "What happens if I can't control it? What happens if in the middle of a battle with the Weres I go dog?"

"That's not going to happen. And even if it did, if you were on our side to start with, you'd still be on our side, fur, fangs and all."

Slade grunted. It wasn't much reassurance. Achilles and Dmitri were humoring him, but he knew the council would have the final say. "Let's just hope it works that way." But even as he said the words, deep down, he doubted it. He was caught in between, at risk of belonging nowhere and to no one. And the second full moon in a month, a blue moon—more powerful than a regular full moon—was two days away. The clock was ticking.

Chapter 15

Slade returned to the security center as soon as he could tear himself away from Dmitri's well-intentioned pep talk. He'd heard enough. The proof would be in how the others acted toward him when they found out he was mixed blood, a half-breed.

He transported into the room and found Raina alone sitting in a chair, her feet propped up on the conference table. "Where'd everybody go? I thought you'd have had all kinds of information out of Ty by now."

She stood and crossed her arms, her eyes dark with disapproval. "So now the Were has a name?"

Slade winced. He had been just as bad as the other vampires when it came to prejudice against the shifters. He stepped toward her, placing a hand on her waist and raising her chin with the crook of his finger to gaze into her eyes. "You're right. But this is war for us and we weren't the ones who declared it."

She nodded, placing her cheek against his chest. The moldy, musty odor of sorrow tinged the air around her. "I feel like I'm stuck in the middle and I don't like it."

He got that. Boy, did he ever. But he was still just as stuck as she was, perhaps more so. He wrapped his arms around her, holding her. "What happened to him?"

"He never woke up. Achilles took him to see Dr. Chamberlin."

Slade ran his fingers in a gentle up-and-down pattern on her back, trying to soothe her. Somehow, making Raina calm helped him relax, as well. "How are you doing?"

"Okay." Raina lifted her head, her gaze connecting with his. "What about you? How did it go with the council?"

Slade shifted his weight from foot to foot, uncomfortable even talking about it. "They let me off with a warning."

"It's about your Were heritage, isn't it?"

His throat seemed to swell shut, refusing to let the words form, so he nodded.

She nibbled at her bottom lip between small, white, even teeth, making it stain a darker rose as her blood rose to the surface. His fangs began to throb as he thought of kissing her, of touching her bare skin. "Looks like we're both in no-man's land even among our own people," she said softly.

Her gentle words seeped into him, a warm, soothing balm that he craved like sunshine after he'd first transitioned. He wanted to fill himself up with her warmth, her steady surety. If he'd been certain they'd be alone in the security center he would have gladly made use of the conference table, but as unstable as things were, he planned to play things safe from here on out.

He brushed his lips against hers and she softened, leaning into him, her hands sliding up his chest to curve around his neck and tangle in the hair at his nape. Deep in her eyes Slade glimpsed something that humbled him completely—a sympathetic soul. Without a word he knew she understood him.

The air in the room shifted, changing with static electric charge as three columns of dark swirling particles formed into the remainder of the security team. James with his blue, piercing eyes and sharp features was flanked on either side by Mikhail, built like a Russian tank, and Titus, whose dark eyes sparked with curiosity.

Slade's shoulders tensed. News traveled fast when everyone could communicate by thought.

"Don't you people ever just walk somewhere?" Raina said, irritation lacing her tone as she pulled away from him.

James laughed, looking at Mikhail and Titus on either side of him. "If you've got skills, why not use them? Am I right or am I right?" He put his hands out palms up and got high fives from the vampires on either side of him. The security team members spread out in a semicircle around Slade and Raina.

James took an exaggerated inhalation. "Ooh. You

smell that, Mikhail? Honey and roses. I'd say Donovan's been busy working on an imprint."

"Donovan's always had a way with the donors," Mikhail answered, his pale green gaze eyeing Raina, then darting to Slade as if he were looking for a physical manifestation of the imprint forming between them.

Raina drew closer to him and slipped her hand into his. Slade gave it a reassuring squeeze. He knew that since he'd marked her no other would touch her. It was an inviolable clan law. But that didn't mean he wouldn't beat down all three of his fellow vampires if they so much as flashed a fang in her direction.

"She's *not* a donor. She's a fellow mortal officer, so show a little respect."

Mikhail locked gazes with him in challenge, crossing his arms over his massive barrel chest. "You want to make me, half-breed?"

"Interesting you should bring up respect. We heard through the grapevine that you've got a flea problem." James snickered.

Slade glared at his fellow security team member and turned his back on him, drawing Raina along with him. "Screw you, Crawford."

"I'm actually surprised you survived the transformation when they turned you from a Shyeld into a full vampire," Titus added. "I didn't think there'd be enough human DNA left if you were a shifter."

While intellectually Slade had expected their taunts when the other vampires of the clan found out, it still stung. The clan had been the only thing close to a family he'd had in all the time he could remember and the thought of losing his place here, his connection to the vampire world and becoming an outcast, was more than he could bear. Deep down in his gut Slade knew that Achilles and Dmitri were simply humoring him out of friendship.

He rounded on James, shoving him back hard in the chest and pointing a finger at them. "Look, I didn't ask for this. Up until last week I thought I was full-blood vampire, same as the rest of you."

James put up his fists, daring Slade to take a swing with a tip of his chiseled chin. "You wanna go, Dogbert, let's go."

He should have just walked away. He should have been able to ignore their gibes, but he was too tangled up inside, not knowing what would happen and if the council was already creating a contingency plan for his removal from the clan. He released Raina's hand. Set on edge he bunched up his shoulders and raised his fist, throwing a quick jab at James, followed by a hard left hook. James grunted, then glared at Slade, and spit out a dark stream of ichor.

Raina skittered back, her hips bumping into the hard edge of the conference table as the vampires traded blows, filling the room with the sound of flesh hitting flesh. She glared at the other two vampires.

"Stop this!" she pleaded. Mikhail and Titus blatantly ignored her, both of them cheering the fight on.

James plowed a fist into Slade's nose with a sickening crunch that caused a spray of warm ichor across the table. Raina squeaked and scrambled out of the way.

Slade grunted and took one unstable step backward, then rolled his shoulders and tucked down, darting forward and pounding James with a rapid series of hits to the midsection that were so fast his fists seemed a blur. James doubled over at the assault. Raina turned away, unable to bear it. She saw the blur of dark particles gathering by the door, ignored by the men in the room.

"Attention!" Achilles roared. Everyone stopped dead in their tracks. "What the hell is going on in here?"

"Just blowing off a little steam playing with the dog," James replied sarcastically, then wiped the back of his hand across his mouth, smearing a dark stream of ichor that dribbled at the corner. Despite the fighting, neither of them were breathing hard, then Raina remembered they didn't need to breathe.

"That's enough. Get back to your posts. Donovan, you come with me." Achilles glanced over at Raina. "You, too, Officer Ravenwing."

Slade stepped into line behind his commander. Raina laid a hand on his back and he shrugged it off. Deep down a little bit of her shriveled in response. The door to the security center closed with a heavy thunk behind them.

"Crawford giving you shit?"

"Nothing I couldn't have beat out of him."

Achilles grunted. "Maybe another time. Right now we've got bigger issues. The Were finally came around."

Slade instantly sobered. His long stride matched Achilles and Raina had to jog along to keep up with the vampires as they turned down another brick-and-concrete hallway. Her memory was fuzzy, but she recalled seeing the rusted-out bathtub and realized they were headed in the direction of the atrium. "Did he say anything?" Her voice wobbled with her motion.

"Only that we've got less than two nights until all hell breaks loose around here. Eris is planning on calling down the blue moon," Achilles said, his voice betraying his tension.

Raina knew a blue moon was the second full moon in a month. They weren't that uncommon. But what she didn't understand was what difference it could possibly make and what the goddess planned to do. "What's calling down the moon?"

Slade glanced back over his shoulder at her and grabbed her hand as they took a sudden turn she nearly missed. "Know how the moon pulls the tides?"

"Yeah?" She glanced down at his hand, seeing the dark color of ichor drying on his knuckles.

"It's water responding to the pull of the moon. She controls the moon, she can control the water."

"You mean like she might cause a tsunami or flood or something?"

He shook his head. "Worse. Way worse."

"Like what?"

"The human body is about seventy percent water. What do you think?"

Cold fear fisted through Raina, squeezing the air out of her lungs. "What can we do to stop her?"

Achilles pushed open the doors to the atrium and crossed it in ground-eating strides as he headed for a small receptionist stand at the far side near the rock wall waterfall. Raina and Slade followed on his heels. "We've got to get the Weres to cooperate," Achilles said. "Ty and his pack believe that she's the moon goddess—they don't know she's the goddess of chaos."

"She's been masquerading as some other goddess?" Raina asked.

"Diana, goddess of the hunt," Slade said.

Achilles caught Slade's gaze. "Bingo." He turned to the receptionist. "Get me Dmitri. Tell him we are with the shifter."

Her dark bobbed hair swung around her cheeks as she nodded. "Yes, Commander."

Achilles swung around the receptionist stand, Slade right by his side, pulling Raina along the hallway with frosted panes of glass on one side and a wall painted a soothing sage-green punctuated with black-and-white pictures on the other.

"Where are we?" Raina asked.

"Clan medical complex," Achilles said without emotion as he beelined to the end of the hall toward a set of white double doors. "Dr. Chamberlin has revived the Were and treated his injuries. Seems last time you two were up there, you did some damage. The Weres don't heal as fast as we do."

"So how is Were cooperation going to stop Eris?" Slade asked as they passed through the double doors into a sterile white laboratory with stainless-steel countertops. The smell of antiseptic and industrial cleaner tweaked Raina's nose.

Achilles kept moving. "This way. He's in Beck's office." They approached the closed door that bore the nameplate Dr. Rebecca Chamberlin-Stefanos, and Achilles put his hand on the doorknob, then stopped for a second. "If we can get their help, we can try to trap her. It's been done before, millennia ago."

"It has?" Slade seemed surprised.

"Long before your time."

"How do you even know this stuff?"

Achilles speared Slade with a hard, level gaze that spoke volumes. "I'm one of the vampires that trapped her."

He opened the door to his wife's office. Raina couldn't see past the broad set of their shoulders to see what was inside. "How are you feeling?" Achilles asked.

Impatient, Raina squeezed between Achilles and Slade. Ty, barefoot and dressed in faded jeans and a T-shirt, was relaxing on a black leather couch, drinking from a steaming mug. The rich smell of coffee made Raina's stomach grumble. Behind the desk at a countertop was Dr. Chamberlin, her mass of curly auburn hair caught up into a messy bun as she peered through a microscope.

"For a prisoner? I feel tolerable," Ty responded. His dark brown eyes flicked to Slade.

"You're not a prisoner," Achilles said, his tone slightly irritated.

"Oh, then a pawn. Is that more accurate?"

Slade stepped toward the shifter. "Look. This is bigger than Weres versus vampires. Eris could potentially control us all and plunge this world into total chaos."

Ty put down the mug on the glass-topped coffee table in front of him, then rested his elbows on his knees. His dark, shaggy hair was almost shoulder length and swung forward slightly. "You both keep mentioning Eris, but the only goddess who has come to us is the goddess of the moon and the hunt."

"She's tricking you," Raina said quickly. "Like Coyote, making you believe what she wants you to." The shifter's gaze rested heavy and expectant on her.

"And why should I believe you? You were to be our link to the people and you have forsaken your sacred duty."

That tore it. Raina marched up to Ty, forcing him to sit up straight to look up at her. "Look, you miserable fur ball." Raina saw his jaw twitch. "I'm not going to be used by anybody. Not you." She thumped him in the chest with her index finger. "Not the vampires." She hitched her thumb over her shoulder. "And not some whacked-out ancient goddess who gets her jollies out of making everyone else miserable. The question you have to ask yourself is, if there were some way to protect your pack and the people, would you take it?"

His eyes blazed like a forest fire. "Of course I would," he ground out between his clenched teeth. "Loyalty is everything in the pack."

"Then quit being so proud and thinking you know it all and listen to these vampires. They may have a way to capture this deceitful goddess who threatens all of us."

Ty glanced from her to Achilles and then Slade. "You

truly believe you are capable of capturing a goddess? You are immortals, not gods," he said with disdain.

Raina noticed that neither of them rose to the bait. Instead, Achilles shrugged. "I say tomato, you say tamahto. Either way, she's going to end up with egg on her face. I've captured her before, shifter. It's just a matter of knowing her weakness."

A feral light glowed behind the shifter's eyes. "Assuming the Whisperer speaks true, then we have little time for you to make your plans. We should leave now." The shifter stood.

Beside Slade a dark cloud gathered, forming into the broad shoulders of Dmitri. Dr. Chamberlin's office was now crowded shoulder to shoulder with vampires. For a moment Raina thought about how it was almost like having a family meeting at Jake's, everyone close together.

"No one is going anywhere until we have a plan," Dmitri said firmly.

"We've got a plan," Achilles said.

"We just aren't one hundred percent sure it'll work," Slade finished.

Dmitri turned his gaze on Slade. "While Achilles fills me in I want you to take Officer Ravenwing to get something to eat before she falls over. We'll meet back here in two hours."

Chapter 16

Slade sat Raina down on a bar stool at his kitchen island countertop, the black granite glittering under the overhead lights. "I'm not even hungry," Raina protested. Her stomach chose that moment to let out a loud, gurgling growl.

Slade gave her an I-know-you're-lying look as he phased an inch-thick New York steak, some garlic, olive oil, a large potato in foil and a bag of salad.

She glanced at the food and her stomach pinched uncomfortably. "Okay, maybe I'm hungry, but I can't eat. My stomach gets upset when I'm upset."

"The thought of going up against the goddess bothers you that much? Not surprising," he said as he pulled out a frying pan from the cupboard, lit up the gas stove, prepped the steak with a smear of olive oil and garlic and set about cooking it.

As a pragmatist, she didn't want to think about goddesses—real or mythical. If mythical they couldn't be a problem, if real… Raina took an appreciative sniff. The smell of the searing steak and garlic made the back of her mouth start to ache as it watered, and set off another loud grumble from her midsection. She shook her head and pushed a fist to her stomach, trying to get it to quiet down.

For a man who didn't need to eat, he seemed to know his way around a kitchen pretty darned well.

Raina's stomach pinched a little harder at the thought that Slade had done this for other women before her. The black silk sheets on the big bed, a motorcycle in the living room and cooking skills…he had all the bells and whistles of seduction at his fingertips.

"The thing with Eris is going to play out one way or another. I don't have much control over that."

"Then what upset you?" Slade pulled apart the salad bag and tossed the contents into a bowl, mixing in the other little packets of cheese, nuts and dressing that came with the salad kit. He did it so effortlessly, as if cooking her a meal was the most natural thing in the world. She wished she could do something just as simple, just as meaningful, to nurture him.

"Watching your team members lash out at you like they did." She met his gaze, and her mouth dried at the heated look he was giving her. "They were just words, Slade. You know that. Those morons were just having a laugh at your expense because they thought they were being funny. I could tell that they like and respect you. They didn't say those things to be mean."

The steak sizzled as he flipped it over. She could see there was mix of seething anger and fear in the depths of his eyes. "I wish that's all it was." He rubbed the edge of his jaw where he'd taken a few punches. She was still surprised he hadn't bruised at all from the fight.

"Damn," he muttered savagely. "I knew this was going to happen."

"They aren't going to turn their backs on you. They'll be there when the time comes for the showdown." She reached for his hand, but he withdrew it. Raina pushed away the hurt feeling it caused. He wasn't pulling away from just her. He was pulling away from everybody. She could tell.

Slade snorted. "Only because they'll follow orders, not because they give a shit what happens to me."

"I don't think—"

"You heard them," he cut her off impatiently. He phased a black plate and took the steak from the pan. "And those are men I considered friends. Guys whose asses I saved a time or two. Who saved mine." His gaze connected with hers. "If they're taking the fact that I'm a half-breed this way, what chance do you think I stand against the clan council? If I shift even once, they're going to toss me out of the clan the minute I step a toe back in the complex."

She folded her arms on the counter. "You should have a little more faith in them. Achilles still trusts you. And from the looks of it so does that Dmitri guy, as well as Kristin and Dr. Chamberlin. I think that says how much they value you a lot more than you realize. I understand how you feel, I really do. But give them a chance to sort through how they're feeling. I think your team members' reaction to the news was knee-jerk—and to be honest, I think fear plays a big part in how all of you are reacting, which is only natural."

Slade sighed, the sound heavy and full of pain. "You don't understand." He split open the foil and the potato with a knife, then gave it a slight squeeze so that the steaming white insides were exposed. A dollop of white sour cream and a pale yellow chunk of butter appeared on top along with a sprinkle of chives that seemed to rain out of thin air. It amazed her that he could materialize the ingredients without even thinking about it. Sure they were different, he a supernatural being and her just a mortal, but they were also the same.

Everyone needed someone to love, and someone who loved them. They needed validation and approval and trust. Vampires and mortals weren't different in that, and she suspected neither were the Weres.

He'd been hurt, and yes, scared, because the clan was his family, and he was terrified, Raina knew, because he'd been abandoned once by people who should have loved him. Now it might happen again. Didn't matter if he was a child or an adult—fear of being alone was a scary thought.

"Oh, but I think I do understand. More than you realize. I may not be part of your clan, but I can see how much being part of them means to you. It's your whole identity—Slade, badass vampire."

He gave her a halfhearted grin. "I should put that on a business card." He frowned. "Except I'd have to put half vampire."

Raina groaned in frustration. "Look, what you need to do is stop worrying about the what-ifs or feeling sorry for yourself, and realize that you've got a connection here, just like I do with my family and my people. That isn't going to just go up in smoke if you happen to change your form temporarily."

He pushed the plate with the steak and potato and the bowl of salad toward her, materializing a fork and steak knife for her in one hand and a napkin in the other, and handing it to her.

"That's not what the council said. One shift. Just one, and I'm outta here.... You better eat up."

Raina looked down at the meal he'd made her, then met his gaze. Saw the banked pain there, and felt an answering pain deep inside. "There's so much more to you than any of them can ever know. And if those stupid vampires are going to be prejudiced against you for something that isn't your fault, then they didn't deserve to have you fighting beside them." She lifted her gaze, connecting with his tawny one. "Thank you."

Not responding to her championship, he shoved his fingers in his front pockets. "No big deal." But it was to her. It showed he cared, not just about the inferno that roared between them physically, but about her as a person. She suspected he didn't let many people this close.

She cut the steak and took a bite. It melted in her mouth as she chewed and made her whole body sit up and take notice. She didn't realize how long she'd gone without eating something other than a handful of trail mix or some other prepacked meal. She swallowed. "This is amazing. I thought you didn't cook."

He tilted his head to the side and raised one dark brow. "I said I don't often have a reason to."

"And feeding me gave you an excuse?"

"Only fair seeing as how you fed me first," he said with a smile. "Now eat up. Can't have you going into a battle on an empty stomach."

Raina tucked in, eating the creamy potato and enjoying the crunch of the salad. The only thing that would make the meal utterly perfect was a glass of wine.

By her hand a wineglass appeared and crimson wine flowed from some invisible bottle, filling it. She speared him with a glance. "You reading my mind again, Donovan?"

His lips twitched. "I thought if we were on friendly enough terms, you wouldn't mind."

Raina reached out, picked up the glass and took a sip. She could get used to this. She stopped in midsip, shocked at the thought. Since when had badass vampires become her type? She gazed over the edge of her glass, staring at the man looking intently back at her. Suddenly that indefinable wildness that seemed to cling to Slade like cologne made a lot of sense. He wasn't just some vampire. He was utterly unique.

She set down the glass and got up from the bar stool, walking slowly up to him. Slade welcomed her next to him, placing his large hands on her hips and drawing her close. Raina put her hands on the hard planes of his chest.

"You strike me as a kind of guy who likes a little risk."

"Mmm-hmm," he rumbled, and Raina felt the vibration through her fingertips. It set off a chain reaction in her. "Then you have to go into this showdown knowing that shifting is a risk you're willing to take. It's like you told Ty, there's more at stake here than just Weres versus vampires. This isn't a territorial fight. It's a fight for all of us against Eris."

He blew out a long, labored breath, kissing her lightly on the forehead. "You're right," he whispered against her skin.

"Of course I am."

He gave a small laugh and lifted his head, giving her a half smile that softened his eyes. He reached out, caressing her cheek with the back of his fingers. "You're something else, you know that?"

"What I know is I'm not vampire."

A deeper light lit in his eyes and yearning filled his voice. "You could be if you wanted to."

Raina grasped his hand at her cheek and held it. "If I could change anything in all of this, it would be that I get to end up with you. But we're from two very different worlds and nothing, not even defeating Eris, is going to change that. You have your clan and I have my people." It killed her to say it, but she had no intentions of leading him on. She couldn't leave her tribe any more than he could stop being a vampire.

He closed his eyes, his face taut with pain, then hung his head, touching his forehead to hers. "You're right. I know that. It's just that I've never felt more like myself than when I'm with you."

Raina felt as though her heart was fracturing. Heartache hurt, just plain old hurt. Being with him seemed so right, and yet their time together was slipping through her fingers every second that ticked closer to the showdown with the Weres, and ultimately Eris.

She realized right then and there that the whole time she'd been trying to care for those around her, she'd neglected herself. Her wants, her desires, had always been tempered by the needs of her people and her responsibilities, even when she didn't believe in all the hocus-pocus about being a Whisperer. Now that she was faced with the facts that her ancestors where Weres, and she was the connection between her people and the shifters, it seemed an all too real obligation. And she'd never asked for any of it. Slade was the first person who didn't ask anything of her other than for her to be precisely who she was.

"Slade Donovan Blackwolf, is that your way of saying you love me?"

"Love is a dangerous thing, Raina. It's like a loaded gun pointed straight at your heart. Somebody else always has their finger on the trigger."

"You're not answering the question, Donovan."

His hand on her hip tightened a fraction and his eyes filled with intensity. "Yeah, nature girl. I love you."

Her mouth curled into a provocative smile. "Prove it."

Slade pulled her close and slanted his mouth over hers, pouring into the kiss everything he hadn't said.

Didn't have a clue *how* to say. The emotion filling him was golden and bubbled like fine champagne. He cupped her cheek as he tasted her need, tasted her love for him. He caressed the soft, warm skin of her cheek. He admired her strength and resolve. How she was funny and sarcastic and mouthy and perfect. How he ached bone deep at the thought of them going their separate ways when this was over.

Without breaking the kiss, he lifted her, placing her up on the island counter. Raina wrapped her arms around his neck and her legs around his waist, her fingers threading through his hair. Need, heady and scented with strawberry and warm female flesh, rolled off her. She kissed him back with everything in her as if he were the last sip of air and she were drowning.

She entangled herself with him in every way possible. Mentally. Physically—every piece of him was engaged in loving her.

Her mouth lush and inviting, her body supple and soft, tempted him to forget who he was and what was happening around them, just to indulge in this one perfect, blissful moment with her lips clinging to his.

With the clarity of a lightning bolt arcing across a dark sky, Slade suddenly realized that he would do anything, be anything, to keep her by his side.

Slade, Dr. Chamberlin's voice invaded his mind, just when he wanted to shut the outside world out most. *You need to report to my office in the clinic in five minutes. We still haven't given you that shot yet.*

Raina pulled back, aware that he'd lost his focus for an instant. "What's wrong?"

Slade shook his head. "Nothing. Just getting paged by the doctor for my shot."

She eyed him, her fingers absently stroking the back of his head in a soothing touch. "Don't you ever get tired of people in your head? I mean, it's cool and all that you can talk to one another with thought, but I'd get tired of having no privacy."

He gave her a quick kiss on her swollen lips. "Believe me, there are times when it's a huge pain in the ass. But there's nothing I can do about it. It's just part of the gig."

Her legs dropped to bracket his hips, and she kept one arm looped around his neck, the other absently stroking his chest. "Are all vampires like that?"

"Nope. Most can block if they choose, but not those of us on the security team. Part of the job requirement so we can be accessed at all times."

The tip of Raina's warm, wet tongue slid over the dent in his chin and crossed his bottom lip. "Sure we can't ignore her a little longer?"

He dipped his head for another searing kiss and hugged her tight, swinging her off the counter. "She'll just make Achilles call me and then I'll have both of them in my head making demands."

"Then I guess we better get you to your doctor's appointment." She sighed.

Slade transported them both to Dr. Chamberlin's offices. "You rang?" he said with a touch of sarcasm in his voice.

Dr. Chamberlin took a slight sniff of the air and arched a brow. "Honey and roses. Was I interrupting something?" Color crept into Raina's cheeks. Dr. Chamberlin was nice enough to ignore it and move on. "I've got your medication ready." She picked up a syringe and tapped it twice, pushing the plunger so that a thin stream of black liquid squirted out the tip. "Put out your arm," she instructed.

Slade hesitated a moment.

"What's in it?" Raina asked.

He eyed the syringe. He didn't particularly care for needles. Truth was he hated them. There'd been so many times he'd seen people shooting up when he was a kid that it had indelibly imprinted on his brain a dislike of the things.

"A concoction of my own design. I'm hoping it'll keep Slade from shifting if his moon sickness gets worse."

Reluctantly, Slade stuck out his arm and looked away. He didn't want to look like a complete wuss in front of Raina, but he couldn't stand to see Dr. Chamberlin stick the needle in his vein, either. Dr. Chamberlin swabbed the bend in his arm with a cold, wet cotton ball that smelled of rubbing alcohol, then pierced his skin. The flow of the liquid from the syringe hurt slightly, but it was the feeling of the needle in his skin that made him feel sick. Ironic, really, considering he didn't mind poking his fangs into people. He was just thankful he wasn't sweating.

The needle slipped from his skin and she put a dry cotton ball over the spot and bent his arm, wedging the bit of fluff between his forearm and his biceps.

"That should do it."

"Thanks, Doc."

"Don't thank me yet, let's see if it works first," she said as she threw the syringe in a sharps box on the wall. "I think Achilles and Dmitri are waiting for you in the security center to brief everyone before you head out."

Slade nodded and grasped Raina about the waist. "Ready to fly?"

She smiled at him. "Ready when you are." Together they disappeared in a dark mist.

A few seconds later they reappeared in the security center. Ty was seated on Achilles's right and the other security members on his left. Dmitri was at the head of the table. Two chairs had been left open for them and they quickly took their seats.

"This is to be a diplomatic mission. Our first order of business is to convince the Weres, with Ty's help, that we have a common enemy. And if *she* isn't defeated, a truce or all-out war between vampires and Weres will be moot. We need to band together to fight Eris. We'll be taking Ty back to his pack and trying to meet with Bracken to discuss Eris and her deception. The goal is to see if we can get their cooperation in trapping Eris."

"Bracken is going to want proof," Ty said.

Dmitri glanced at him. He leaned over and pressed his fists to the tabletop. "I know. Problem is the only way we can get proof is either A, summon Diana and hope she shows, which is highly unlikely, or B, taunt Eris into revealing herself." Dmitri nodded to Achilles. "Achilles is going to fill you in on the particulars."

Achilles stood, maintaining his position between Ty

and the other members of the security team. "We'll be going in as a group. Slade and Officer Ravenwing will take point and go in with Ty. We're serving as their backup on this one."

"Aren't they going to be pissed we took him?" James pointed out, tapping his fingers on the top of the conference table.

Achilles glared at James. "He's agreed to tell them he came along willingly, to help us in this process. Neither side wants to have their own hurt, especially if this is all just a setup by Eris. Ty, Ravenwing and Donovan, you three will transport in to the edge of the Wenatchee Pack territory and wait for us to join you. Ty has agreed to take you to the pack den to meet with Bracken. James, Titus, Mikhail, you three will be with me, posted as lookouts to make sure nothing gets out of hand. Everybody know where you're supposed to be?" Around the table everyone nodded. "Good. Dismissed."

People rose from their chairs. Raina grabbed hold of Slade's hand as Ty skirted the table toward them.

The Were gave Slade a challenging look. "You brave enough to go in alone with just me and the Whisperer, vampire?" he said, low and quiet, next to Slade's ear.

"I'm good. You think Bracken will listen before he takes a bite out of us?"

"He's not going to be easy to persuade but he can be if you present enough evidence. And you have the Whisperer with you. That'll help."

Slade didn't want to think about what might happen if Bracken figured out who he really was. "Ready?" he asked Ty.

"In a moment." Ty bent his head, and the hair rose on Slade's arm as the energy around him changed. He reached out and grabbed Ty by the shoulder, knowing he was planning on wolfing-out in front of the vampires. Ty glared at him, his brown eyes piercing.

"Don't make this any harder than it already is. You can shift when we get there," Slade said, warning infusing his voice.

Ty glanced at the others in the room. James muffled his chuckle. Mikhail's eyes narrowed and Titus rubbed his hand lightly over his fist. Ty rolled his shoulders, the muscles in his jaw twitching as he ground his teeth. The tension in the room doubled, growing thick and smelling like the cedar and musk typical of too much testosterone circulating in a limited space. Slade could tell Ty had wanted to psych out the others with a little freak show. He still didn't get they were on the same side.

"He's right," Raina added. "If you want us to trust you, you've got to do the same."

Ty gave one curt nod and narrowed his eyes. "Fine. Then take me home, vampire."

Slade wrapped a hand around Ty's bicep and his other arm around Raina's waist and all three of them pulled inside out as they transported back to the bluff below Red Top Mountain.

Chapter 17

Dawn broke slowly over the mountaintops, burnishing the snow on the high alpine peaks to a brilliant gold. Down in the lower elevations, mist clung eerily in the creases and dips of the sleeping valley, lingering among the shadowy darkness of trees. To Raina, the wooded bluff beneath Red Top Mountain looked...forlorn.

The early-morning shadows, the mist, the semidarkness of a day not fully realized, gave a sense, at least to her mind, of fearful anticipation. Her skin prickled in goose bumps from the chilly morning air, and she briskly rubbed her hands on her arms. In the confines of the clan complex it had been difficult to discern night from day or even the temperature outside. Now she wished she'd thought to tell Slade she'd need a warm jacket. Or maybe, she thought with a shiver of foreboding, what she needed was Were-proof body armor? Underneath her fingers she suddenly felt leather instead of skin as a jacket, lined with something soft. She glanced at Slade and he gave her a slight nod and a wink.

Ty grumbled beneath his breath something about vampires and gave her an arch glance. He wore only the T-shirt and faded jeans provided to him by Dr. Chamberlin. "There's a reason why this is our territory. We're made for it." He lowered his head, his long hair obscuring his features and Raina watched in horrified fascination as he transitioned from man to beast.

The grotesque cracking and sucking sounds that accompanied the breaking, shifting and reformation of bone, muscle, skin and hair was revolting but efficient. His jaw, nose and ears elongated into a lupine form. Hair spread down from his scalp, covering his back and shoulders, and sprouted rapidly into a thick pelt over his entire body. His fists curled, forming paws, and his spine grew longer to form a swishing tail.

She just hoped she never had to witness Slade do that. It looked painful.

Ty shook himself, ridding his gleaming thick gray fur of the last shreds of the clothing that had burst apart into fragments. "Much better," he rumbled in wolf, his pink tongue moving as he panted.

"Dude, that's disgusting," Slade said under his breath.

Ty gazed at him and yipped. "There's nothing as solid as four feet on the earth."

"How far are we from the pack den?" Raina used

the yips and rolling, rumbling sounds that formed the Weres' communication.

Slade raised his nose to the air and inhaled. "About five hundred yards up the face of the mountain, that way." He pointed.

Ty blinked, his one ear twitching back and forth in agitation. "You're good, vampire."

Slade didn't dare tell Ty the reason why. Being half Were had advantages when you were tracking them. It also had disadvantages when the alpha of the pack you were about to the visit wanted you dead.

Behind them, four spirals of dark particles formed into the remainder of the clan security team that blended back into the shadows of the trees, avoiding the rising sun. Achilles gave Slade a thumbs-up. *Good luck. And watch your back,* he said, his words echoing in Slade's skull.

Slade nodded. "Let's head out. The others will stay here and wait for us to return."

Ty took up the lead, trotting through the ground fog like a silent shadow. He was fast enough that Slade could keep up, but Raina had to jog. "Slow down," he admonished Ty. "She's only human."

Still running, the Were glanced back, his brown eyes amused. "That's where you're wrong, vampire. She's a Whisperer, a soul-link between our kind and our people."

"She can't be both."

"The same virus that runs in us runs in her, as well,

but she won't transform until she has mated with the alpha."

That stopped Slade dead in his tracks. "What?"

"She's been destined to be the pack's alpha female since she was chosen to mate with Bracken."

Oh. Hell. No. Not gonna happen. The thought of Raina "mating" with anyone but himself made Slade's ichor run cold.

Slade lowered his voice. Raina was a good fifteen feet back as she jogged to catch up. "Does she know?"

Ty shook his massive head, making his ruff fan out. "No Whisperer is told until they are brought before the alpha. Most don't wish to be neck bit as they are mated." Amusement danced in the shifter's eyes. "Don't look so worried, vampire. As it is, Bracken might reject her, seeing as how *you've* already bitten her."

Slade mentally berated himself for letting his emotions show so clearly on his face. Normally he was fairly good at hiding such things, but when it came to Raina it was almost impossible. She meant too much to him now to let anything happen to her.

How's it going? Achilles interrupted his thoughts.

So far so good. Nearly there.

Were behaving himself?

Yeah. For the most part. Just found out Raina's position is traditionally mated to the alpha—with or without their consent.

Raina isn't going to go for that.

Neither will I.

Stay vigilant. If you sense something is going down you call in backup ASAP. Got me?

He lifted his head to smell the air. Were. Half a dozen at least. Fast approaching from the north. *Yes, sir.*

Approach slowly. Ty ordered the other Weres, unaware Slade could hear him too.

Hell, his brain was cluttered with unspoken conversations.

Raina caught up, then braced her hands on her knees and doubled over to catch her breath. "Thanks for waiting for me," she panted.

"Sorry," Slade offered, senses alert as the scent of wet fur crept closer. "You doing okay?" He kept his voice casual and his eyes moving. It took everything in him not to go for the throwing star in his front pocket. He relaxed his shoulders and spread his feet. Ready, he hoped, for anything.

Raina wiped her brow with the back of her hand. "Hey, I'm warmer now," she said then smiled.

That was his woman.

The hair on the back of Slade's neck lifted in warning. And seconds later out of the mists hugging the base of the trees came ten wolves. They slipped into a circle around their small group, hemming them in. Slade placed a hand over his throwing star. Just in case…

He waited for Ty to tell them that he and Raina were on a diplomatic mission. Instead, the Were looked at his brethren, connecting with them, talking to them in the same way Slade talked to his brother vampires. *The Whisperer wants to see Bracken.* Ty circled Raina's legs, then used his large head to butt her forward.

She turned to glance at Slade, and he gave her a small nod. Despite her training he could see her shaking, her skin a shade paler than normal. She grasped the leather jacket he'd phased for her more tightly about herself and he had a sudden desire for his arms to be around her instead.

Don't show any fear.

Matching her pace to Ty's, she walked forward.

Slade made to follow, but the pack closed ranks.

Several growled a warning, black lips peeling back over bared sharp teeth. Slade took in the Were, calculating in an instant their strength by numbers. Without being able to physically touch Raina, he couldn't transport her out of danger. All his senses were on hyperalert as he watched tails and ears for any signs of attack.

He could move lightning fast, but faster than a determined pack of Were?

He didn't like the way the Were sniffed her. And he could see by Raina's stiff posture that, for all her bravery, she wasn't enjoying the experience, either. Her cheeks, already ruddy from the cold, pinked up even more. He could hear the hard pounding of her blood zinging through her veins and see the way she was holding her breath to regulate her fear. Fear heated her skin, filling his senses with the scent of strawberries.

None of his thoughts manifested on his face. He stood there. Cool, calm and in control. But inside was another matter.

"Take the Whisperer to Bracken. Kill the vampire," Ty ordered.

His gut instinct had known this was going to happen. But Slade still clenched his teeth. Damn double-crossing bastard. Diplomatic mission his ass, this was an ambush. Slade didn't hesitate, not when Raina's safety was at stake. *Achilles. Backup, now!*

Behind Slade, the four vampires instantly materialized.

Furry heads jerked up, ears pitched, and keen, feral eyes tracked the new arrivals. Hair raised, the Weres rushed them. The pounding of large paws on the earth thundered in the cold morning air. Fast. My God, they were fast. Just a blur of fur.

And then they were on him. Before he could brace for the attack, twin paws slammed into Slade's chest. Pain exploded across his right shoulder from behind. Knocked off balance, Slade shoved the wolf away and stumbled and fell to his knees as daggers of ice cut through his body. The battle raged about him, a chaos of flying fur and fangs. Pain radiated through his veins, chilling him to the core and immobilizing him. His throat seized up and he couldn't even speak. He lay there, useless, helpless, keeping his eyes on Raina until his world went black.

A scream rose up in Raina's throat as Slade fell. Blurs of fur leaped at the other vampires, forcing them to close ranks back to back.

Three of the wolves pushed her forward with their wet noses. She pushed and shoved at them, trying to kick them out of the way in an attempt to get to Slade. The Weres growled and snapped, holding her at bay. When she tried to turn back, two of them latched carefully on to her clothing with their teeth and dragged her away from the fight.

"We trusted you," she yelled at Ty as she staggered to stay on her feet as the wolves pushed and shoved her in the direction they wanted her to go.

His ears flicked back in her direction so she knew he'd heard her, but he refused to turn around. "You asked to see Bracken, didn't you?"

"Not like this, and you know it."

With wolves flanking her on all four sides she had no way to break free and run back to the battle. Curses and screams, growls and yips grew fainter as they moved deeper into the trees.

"What I know, Whisperer, is that you are lucky you are not being shredded apart along with the vampires. Consider yourself fortunate to be chosen."

Her chest felt tight with fear. Now more for Slade than herself. God. Had that Were killed him? Was it possible for him to die from a Were bite?

"I never asked to be the Whisperer," she said, her voice grim.

A rasping chuckle, half bark but human enough, escaped from Ty's throat. "None do."

Bright sunlight, piercing in its intensity, filtered through the branches overhead as the sun rose above the trees. Slade and the others would be hampered in their battle by the brightness.

How badly was Slade hurt? Because he wasn't dead. Raina knew in her aching heart that he *couldn't* be dead. She'd know it, wouldn't she?

Birdsong and the scurry of small animals halted with their passage, the quiet of the woods broken only by the soft padding of large paws on the soft, pine needle–

strewn ground, and the hard *clump-clump-clump* of her boots. Or perhaps that was the fast beat of her heart.

As they approached the broad slabs of reddish stone spiking up from the forest floor, Ty drew up short. At the tip of Red Top Mountain sat a squat lookout tower, precariously balanced on silts, but lower down, in the rocks she could see the edge of a cave.

The other wolves followed Ty's lead and released their hold on her clothing. Ty stepped forward. "Bracken is waiting up on the ridge."

Raina stayed exactly where she was and crossed her arms. "Did Bracken order you to kill the vampires?"

He glanced back at her and blinked. His brown eyes were hiding something. "Bracken ordered me to protect our borders."

Deep down, Raina knew it was more than that. "Don't lie to your Whisperer. You and I both know we came to talk. There was no threat."

He turned on her, pacing back and forth, his hackles raised and his fur raised into a stiff ridge along his spine. "You came to fill Bracken's head with your lies. The moon goddess told us you would."

Oh, no. No. No. Raina's heart raced even faster. *What was this about? Why this sudden change of heart?*

"She also told us of Bracken's mongrel among you," volunteered the brownish wolf beside her.

Raina glanced at the wolf. Ty growled at him. "You speak out of turn."

The brown Were tilted his head, almost rolling over, exposing his underside in a sign of submission.

The breath caught in Raina's throat and her skin

grew clammy as her blood drained from her face. They knew. They knew Slade was Bracken's son and they wanted him dead. Then another thought, even more terrifying, filled her. What would happen when Slade returned for her? She had no doubt he would.

Instead of being the bait in a plan to get the wolves to assist in trapping the goddess, she had become the bait to trap Slade.

Her stomach cramped and her aching heart thumped hard in her chest. In asking Slade to assist her with her job, she was inadvertently going to be instrumental in bringing about his death.

She took in a deep breath through her nose and lifted her chin. "What does Bracken want with me?"

"You are the chosen. The Whisperer. And like every Whisperer before you, you will be the alpha's mate, if he will have you now that you've been contaminated by the vampire," Ty said with a derisive huff.

Raina stopped her mouth from dropping open. "Mate? Nobody said anything about mating with a wolf." If such a thing were even possible, which she doubted. She hoped, *prayed*, wasn't possible. "Not that I was asked, but tell Bracken the answer is a resounding, emphatic *no*. That is *not* going to happen."

Ty turned and stalked toward her, his movements low and threatening. "If you refuse him, Whisperer, then you will die."

Raina swayed slightly, shocked by Ty's words. She refused to accept that Slade being lured to his death and her acceptance of her traditional role as Whisperer or death were her only choices. "Surely Bracken wouldn't want an unwilling mate," she countered with more bravado than she felt.

Ty snickered, a series of small barks. "You obviously don't know Bracken. He enjoys bending others to his will. Now, you will follow me."

Well, Bracken hadn't met her, Raina thought furiously. A nudge of a wolf nose at her bottom goosed her forward. Raina trudged up the hill following Ty, growing more angry with every step.

Focus. Think, she told herself. What did she have that she could use? She had her gun on her belt. Her cuffs. Some pepper spray and extra ammo. Zip ties. Her baton. The special metal chains Achilles had given her both in silver and the funny gold-looking metal he'd called orchalcium that was supposed to hold the goddess the same way the silver seemed to work on Weres and vampires.

They crested the ridge and Raina gasped. Her steps faltered. There, in the mouth of a natural cave carved into the rock, sat the largest wolf she'd ever seen. He was the size of a bull.

His pelt was thick and luxurious and a pure silver. A ragged scar ran down the right side of his muzzle, puckering his silvered fur and narrowly missing his brown eye.

He was surrounded by twelve other wolves, all of which looked expectantly at the newcomers.

She and Ty approached, and Ty bowed his muzzle between his paws.

"Excellent work, Ty. I see you have brought our Whisperer home."

Bracken's great canines, the size of large carving knives, were yellowed with age. Raina's skin crawled with revulsion at the thought of them touching her.

"Come forward, Whisperer," Bracken ordered.

Raina wanted to hold back, but something compelled her to move forward toward the old wolf. She stopped about five feet away, noting that the alpha's paws were huge, twice the size of a normal wolf. How on earth did Slade and the others have a prayer of standing up to something like this?

Bracken took a deep inhalation, then grimaced, his black lip curling back over his massive pointed teeth. "You have been among the vampires. I can smell it on you."

"I didn't realize that was a problem," she said, her voice shaky.

Bracken locked his penetrating gaze on hers. "The only reason we have spared you, Whisperer, is because you did not know any better. Had you been brought to us, then defected to the vampires, the consequences would have been far higher."

Despite the warm sunshine heating her shoulders, Raina shivered. She'd never felt so exposed or alone in her entire life.

"Do I intimidate you, Whisperer?" Bracken's voice was low, rumbly and tinged with pleasure.

Raina forced herself to summon up every measure of training she'd received at the academy. Just because something looked intimidating didn't mean she didn't have some control. They hadn't taken her weapons. She could fight if she needed to. "I just find it kind of hard to imagine you as anything other than an animal when you're sporting a fur coat. It might be easier if you were in your human form," she said in her most authoritative police officer voice.

Bracken's lips widened, a parody of a smile. "You're strong. I like that. It will make you a good alpha female for the pack," Bracken answered. "As a gesture of my good faith, I will change for you, Whisperer."

The huge wolf rose up on his haunches, his massive head tucking down to his chest. This time Raina closed her eyes, not wanting to see the messy, painful-looking process involved in shifting from one form to another. Unfortunately, she couldn't cover her ears without being completely obvious, and she could still hear the disturbing wet pop, crush and squish as his body shifted.

She peeked under her lashes and then opened her eyes wide in surprise. Before her stood a muscular mountain of a man the size of Slade, whose long, dark hair was shaded with silver at the temples. A jagged scar marred his tan right cheek below his piercing brown eyes and a set of scars, four lines parallel to one another stood out white against his chest. And he was very, very naked and big all over.

And he looked so much like Slade that Raina's heart twisted. He was a much older, bitter-looking, harder version of his son. Had Kaycee stayed here, would Slade have become just as haughty and mean-looking? In Bracken's eyes she glimpsed the intelligence and determination that she'd seen in Slade's. Certainly father and son would have butted heads, since Slade chaffed under rules and an alpha demanded nothing less than total submission from his pack members. But both she and Slade weren't part of his pack. Not yet.

At least Raina had expected nudity to accompany the shift this time and tried to keep her eyes level with the old alpha's face, and definitely no lower than his chest. Beside her Ty chuckled in his rough wolf way. She briefly considered kicking him, then thought better of it.

"Is this more acceptable to you, Whisperer?" Bracken asked, slowly walking around her, raking her with his gaze, as if he were inspecting a side of beef.

"The name is Raina Ravenwing."

"Raina. A queen, how fitting. You will do."

"No," she told him firmly. "Sorry. I won't."

"You—won't?" He growled low. "You are the Whisperer. I am your alpha. There was no question involved."

"I have come here on a diplomatic mission to save your people and protect mine. I have not come here as a Whisperer and I have no desire to mate with you." She shuddered. *Live with it.*

She bit back further tart comebacks, knowing it would not improve her situation. She needed to bide her time until Slade returned and figure out a way she could warn him when he did.

Raina purposely schooled her features to feign interest and looked at Bracken through her lashes and quickly added, before he could argue. "I hear you've got a goddess advising you," she murmured. "You must be powerful." Playing to a man's ego always worked on the force. She figured the same rules applied with these furred-up testosterone junkies, as well.

Bracken smiled, his teeth now even and normal rather than jagged, but still just as yellowed. "The moon goddess has shown us much favor. She will be leading a ceremony to cement our presence as leaders among all the people of this area."

Raina bit her lip, stifling a wry smile. Really? He thought she was going to give him all that? Talk about delusional. If she knew one thing from observing humanity as an officer it was that people who offered up great power or rewards in exchange for cooperation usually planned to use someone and then discard those they used.

"And what will that gain you? Have you been over the mountains lately? Lot of traffic."

"No matter. The goddess will command them all to lie at our feet and we shall be their masters. We will be free of the vampires. Free to roam as we will in any form we choose."

Hoo, yeah. He had it bad. All she had to do was keep him talking. "Tell me more," she said sweetly.

Bracken's gaze narrowed, his lip curling slightly. "You've been among the vampires long enough to tell us of their weaknesses."

Raina gave a mirthless little laugh. "And why would I do that?"

"I am told you are a warrior of sorts among your people." Raina remained stock-still as he reached out and touched the gear on her belt. "You've gone to great lengths to learn how to protect them in the human world. It's part of the reason you were not brought before me sooner. We had hoped the training, the time out among humans, would strengthen your skills and responsibility to your people."

"What we? As far as I can tell, you're the only one calling the shots around here. And I've come to tell you that the goddess has been deceiving you. She's not the moon goddess or even the goddess of the hunt. She's Eris, the goddess of chaos, who feeds off pain, panic, fear and agony. She doesn't care if the pack even survives! All she wants is war between you, the vampires and the humans."

"You do not know our moon goddess—the vampires have fed you lies, Whisperer."

"No, they didn't. It's Eris who's been doing all the lying. She's blinded you and your pack to the unpalatable truth. She's using you, and you're not thinking clearly if you believe even half the lies she's told you!"

He chuckled, the rumbling down deep in his muscled chest. He picked up a strand of her hair and sniffed it. "Ah, my Whisperer, you still do not comprehend how closely tied you are to my pack already."

"Well, perhaps it's past time that the ancestors and my people went their separate ways. Things have changed. You can't expect to have the same relationship with humans as you have had with our people for all these centuries. It won't happen. The people in Seattle will fight you, as will the vampires."

Bracken stared deeply into her eyes. "They can't be separated. And it is time for you to take your place among us as the chosen." He turned back to the other wolves, who occupied the mouth of the cave. "Show her your true forms. All of you."

Raina stared, unable to move or speak as the wolves all sat up and began to shift into human forms. They were all faces she recognized. Her aunt Lee, Robbie, Mo's husband, Jake, even her own mother and father. She blinked rapidly and rubbed her eyes, hoping that it was just an illusion. *No. Oh no, no. no.*

Her mother stepped forward, her hand extended palm upward, her long, dark hair flowing over her shoulder and breasts and down past her hips. "We have been waiting for you to join us, Raina, but we wanted you to come to us in your own time."

The words burned right through Raina and the very air seemed to stop moving. Her mother and father, her aunts, the people in town, they'd *known.* Worse, they'd hidden from her. Sure, they'd told her she was the Whisperer, but they'd never explained the rest of what went with it! Fury raced through her, making her shake, her pulse a pounding rush in her ears. "Wait. Just wait a second." She backed away from her mother. "You've known all along I was a shifter?"

Her mother smiled sweetly and nodded. "You've just never been bit. The ancestors are part of the people and the people of the ancestors. It has always been so." The familiar words repeated like a slow drum rhythm in Raina's chest.

Raina stared at her mother. "You lied!" She glared at the others. "All of you lied to me! And now you expect me to be glad about it?" Her life, her entire existence, had been a charade to cover up this more insidious truth. No wonder the people were so insular and had wanted to keep it that way. They had a huge, frightening secret to keep.

"This is a gift," her mother persisted.

Raina rounded on her mother. "This has never been a gift to me, it's been a duty, a burden shoved on me without my asking. My entire life has been a lie!" Raina cried. "Why didn't I learn of this when I was a child?"

Her mother shook her head. "Things did not turn out well for the last Whisperer. We had hoped with time and space to grow older, you'd avoid her mistakes."

Raina's mind spun. Kaycee's mistake had been to fall in love with a vampire, then become one. Well, she'd already gone and fallen love with one damn hot vampire. She was halfway there. She glanced at Bracken and, with lightning clarity, understood Kaycee's choice. While Slade might resemble his father, the two were as different as night and day.

"You should have told me." Raina pushed her fists to her aching temples.

"We told you what you were," her mother said, her voice cautious and even. "But until you were prepared for the bite, there was no reason you needed to know the rest of it. It would have been too big a burden."

"Bullshit! You just didn't want me to tell all of you to go screw yourselves and take off like Kaycee Blackwolf did."

Several of them winced.

She tore her gaze away from her mother and stared at Bracken. "What about those wolves who were fighting the vampires today—are they my people, too?"

He gave one curt nod. Her head pounded. How many of them were people she knew and cared for, as well? And if they went to battle against the vampires, against Eris, how many of her people would die?

"Now that you have learned the truth, Whisperer, it is time for you to become one of us."

Chapter 18

Fighting the agonizing pain that thrummed in every cell the instant he woke, Slade's eyes snapped open to see Dr. Chamberlin and Achilles standing at his bedside. Damn. Double damn. He was in the clan hospital.

"Where the hell is she?" He shoved aside the sheet then almost passed out from the fresh, sharp onslaught of razor-sharp pain that knifed through his shoulder. As he tried to stand, Slade grunted and ground his teeth.

Achilles gripped him by the opposite shoulder, pushing him back against the mattress. The fresh note of forest flora and fauna clung to him. As did the stink of feral Were. The green of hís commander's eyes were as hard as glacial ice. "You're not going to like this."

Slade smacked his hand away as his tension torqued up another notch and he sat up anyway, powered by his need to protect Raina. His hospital pajama top gaped open. "Where. Is. She?"

"The Weres took her. The battle got out of hand. We didn't expect them to ambush us in broad daylight."

His head snapped up. "And you let them take her?"

"We were lucky to drag your ass back here before we were all killed. We underestimated them. They're faster and fiercer than we imagined."

"I'm transporting back. Now." He swung his legs over the side of the bed, but it took considerable effort for him to do so. He was as useless as block of C4 without a fuse. He shot the doctor a puzzled look. "How long have I been out?"

"A few hours."

Slade frowned, his head spinning and his vision blurry. Moon sickness kicking his ass again? He mentally did a body check. No. This was different. Debilitating in a different way. "Why am I so weak? My body's had time to heal. I should be back in fighting form." Yet he wasn't. Not by a long shot.

Dr. Chamberlin glanced at the machines beeping by Slade's head and flipped the chart in her hand to make a notation. "What the hell was Crawford thinking to shoot him like that?" she muttered and shook her head.

"He shot me?"

Achilles frowned. "In the fray he was afraid you'd shift, so he shot you in the back with a silver-tipped DMD. Didn't want to have to figure out which of the Weres we could and couldn't kill because one of them might be you."

Silver and dead man's blood. Gods, no wonder he

hurt so bad. Both were powerful poisons and nervous system inhibitors. He was lucky he hadn't just slumped over like a wet noodle. It bothered but didn't surprise him that James had shot him in the back, literally, because he didn't trust him to be able to control himself.

"Look here, please," Dr. Chamberlin said as she took a penlight and flashed it past his eyes, causing them to dilate with a sharp stab to pierce his brain that immediately faded.

"It ended up being the four of us against twenty Weres." Achilles crossed his arms over his chest and leaned a shoulder against the wall. He did not look happy. "Ty never intended to let us talk to Bracken. Eris must have promised them some pretty big concessions to win their total loyalty like that."

Terror ripped through him in equal measure to the pain freezing his joints and making him feel like he was in the midst of a bout of moon sickness all over again. He focused, trying to transport. All he got was a weak fizzle of sensation. "We have to go. Now."

Achilles shook his head. "It's less than twelve hours before the blue moon. We go back now and we're asking for Eris to squash us."

Slade stiffened. "How long was I out?"

"Six hours."

Beads of moisture popped out on Slade's forehead. Anything could have happened in six hours. He knew without a doubt Bracken would try to force Raina to mate and it wouldn't turn out well.

Slade turned to Dr. Chamberlin and held out his arm, full of intravenous needles taped in place. "Get these things out of me." She obliged, removing the ichor drip and monitoring devices strapped to his arm.

Focused on Achilles and his fear for Raina, he didn't even feel the needles being pulled from his skin. "You said you know how to trap Eris."

Dr. Chamberlin's gaze flicked for an instant to Achilles, her lips pressing together in disapproving line, but she kept silent.

"I do. But she's going to have to be distracted for it to work. If she draws down the moon, she'll be able to control us."

"You, yes. But not the Weres. I think I may have just the advantage we need to beat her."

Achilles stared down at Slade, his eyes blazing. "Not a good idea."

The hospital room suddenly seemed suffocating to Slade. The need to reach Raina dominated all other concerns. It wasn't about *if* he was going to go up against Bracken, but *when*. And with Raina at stake that was going to happen sooner than later.

"I didn't say it was a good idea, just the best that I could come with on the fly." Slade glanced down at his hospital pajamas and phased them away, replacing them with black fatigue pants, a black T-shirt and his favorite boots. Even that much effort made him feel woozy.

"But if you transition—"

He held up a hand, stopping Achilles. "I'm well aware of the consequences, but if it buys us time, then as a last resort I'll do what I have to do. Like Raina said, this is bigger than just us versus them. This is Eris we're talking about. Everybody could get screwed."

"True."

"Well, don't sugarcoat it or anything," Slade said with a grunt.

"Are you dizzy or in pain?" Dr. Chamberlin asked as she took Slade's arm and assisted him off the bed. The room swayed and for a minute it looked like there were two of everybody.

"No problemo," he answered, giving her a thumbs-up that really looked like maybe three or four thumbs.

Dr. Chamberlin raised an eyebrow. "Right." She glanced at Achilles. "Watch him for the next half hour. If he's unstable bring him back. I can't tell if it's the residual effects of the DMD in his system or an increasing reaction to the moon sickness."

"Doesn't matter," Slade muttered. "We've still got a job to do." He pinned Achilles with a gaze that said he refused to take no for an answer. "When does the team leave?"

Achilles shifted his weight uneasily from one foot to the other. "You and I are going in solo."

"What?" For a second he felt deflated all over again. They wouldn't back him up because they feared he'd go dog.

"The others took the brunt of the attack. They're still being treated and fed down the hall."

Slade sighed. Well, perhaps it was more because they were injured than worried. "But they'll be fine," he prompted.

"Yes. But Dmitri has determined this needs to be a stealth operation. If we get an opportunity to subdue Eris, great, but that's not the primary goal. We're to do what we can to get rid of her, even if it means taking out Bracken."

Slade nodded. "And grab Raina."

Achilles's mouth flattened into a firm line. "If it's possible."

"Of course it's freakin' possible."

"Not if they've already bit her and started the transition." Achilles turned on his heel and jerked his head, indicating Slade should walk with him.

Slade rolled his shoulders and stepped out into the hallway with Achilles. "That's a chance I've got to take," Slade said.

They walked in silence down the length of the medical clinic and out past the reception desk to the atrium. Achilles put a hand on Slade's shoulder, stopping him in his tracks, and waited until Slade's gaze connected with his. "Remember, those are her people and she's got a connection to them. She might decide that she'd rather stay where she belongs."

Slade frowned. "Why the change of tune?"

Achilles pulled his hand away, a pensive look crossing his face. "You obviously don't remember Kaycee." He broke eye contact with Slade, and Slade got the curious sensation that Achilles had held back far more than the information about knowing who his mother and father were. "She wanted nothing more than to escape to a different life. She was nothing like Raina," Achilles added.

"Then why in the hell did she go back?"

Achilles's gaze, full of solemnity, locked onto his. "They took you."

A shudder rippled through Slade. "Used me as bait."

Achilles nodded, a softness flitting across his eyes like a memory quickly dismissed. "There was nothing she wouldn't have done for you."

Slade's stomach curled uncomfortably in upon itself as he peered at Achilles, for the first time seeing the tired lines around his eyes. "You say that like you knew her."

For a moment Achilles said nothing, then took a deep breath. "I was her maker. The vampire who helped her become one of us."

Shock swelled his throat closed, making it hard to push out the words. "So you and she—" Slade said, then waved his hand, brushing off his question. "Never mind."

"Kaycee was an amazing person. I was there when you were born."

"You what?" Slade backed up a pace. "My God! Are you my surrogate father?"

"No. More like your uncle. Close family ties, but not your father. Kaycee and I were friends, not lovers. She only asked for one thing from me after you were born. She wanted me to watch out for you, give you the choice to become one of us, if you wanted it. I think she knew what would happen if she ever returned to the pack."

The room started to spin again. He needed to sit down. Thinking of what had happened to his mother made him worry about what was happening that very moment to Raina. Slade settled on the edge of one of the cushy white armchairs in the atrium lounge area. "So the whole Shyeld thing—"

"We came to get you the minute she called us telling us they were going to execute her. We brought you to Seattle, but before we could get you into the complex, you took off."

A vision of running in the dark, the streetlights blurring through the tears flashed across his mind. He'd slept that night in an alley, curled against a doorway.

"It took us two years of searching to find you among the mortals."

Slade peered at Achilles. "She's the reason the council wouldn't let you create or mentor any other females until the doc."

Achilles nodded, his eyes sad. He'd obviously cared for Slade's mother and had taken her death hard on a number of levels. The scent of regret, metallic and sharp, permeated the air. "The council held me responsible for Kaycee's death. Not exactly a stellar mark on a vampire who's supposed to have security locked down."

"Why didn't you tell me any of this sooner?"

Achilles shrugged. "We glamoured you after we found you. Tried to help you forget everything you had witnessed in the hope that it would spare your mind the trauma."

Slade nodded. "I want to hear every detail about my mother and about my past, but right now I have more immediate concerns." He paused, swallowing hard. His next words stuck in his throat because he really didn't want to say them out loud. "You really think Raina will want to stay?"

Achilles crossed his arms. "Can't say. You know her better than I do. What do you think?"

Slade rose, phased himself a leather jacket and a pair of wraparound sunglasses. "I think we're riding to a rescue."

Chapter 19

Slade and Achilles transported to the edge of the Wenatchee Pack's territory, both in flux. They'd agreed that being invisible was necessary from the outset. The Weres would have lookouts posted at the perimeter, so avoiding detection would be their first challenge. Staying invisible was their second. Slade could only hold a flux for an hour, Achilles maybe three, because he'd had longer to build his skills.

Which way to the den? Achilles trusted Slade's tracking abilities. Slade was grateful to have the powerful vampire with him.

Their mental vampire communication bettered their odds of success. The fact that he could also "hear" Were communications was a godsend.

Slade closed his eyes and focused on picking out the

distinct odor of feral wet dog, pungent wood smoke and the subtle currents of Raina's strawberry scent that rode the wind.

North by northeast. Five hundred yards up the ridge by those rocks. The smoke from a campfire smudged the sky. There, shifters were clearly unafraid of detection. *Don't get too confident, you bastards,* Slade cloaked his thoughts. *You have my woman. Think I won't come get her?* Or did they hope he would? Was Raina bait for a trap?

He and Achilles expected a trap. Hell, they were ready for it. Bring it on!

You approach from the east, Achilles told him. *I'll approach from the west.*

Slade slipped through the trees less than a shadow. The sky had crowded with thick thunderclouds during the latter half of the day, making the setting sun only discernible through the overall darkening of the sky. Lightning flashed over the distant high peaks and thunder rolled and rumbled. The storm was coming, in more ways than one.

Slade swiftly scaled the rock, careful where he put each foot and handhold so as not to leave a mark or make a sound.

"The moon will rise soon." Slade recognized Ty's voice.

"Good. Prepare the Whisperer. The goddess can join us in celebrating her return to the pack."

If Slade had a heart, it would've jolted. Was he too late?

On his belly, he crawled to peer over the edge of the

red rocks, to the tableau in the clearing below. Close to thirty Weres gathered around a large fire that crackled and popped, sending up a shower of red-orange sparks into the darkening sky. Off to one side was an X created from two peeled timbers lashed together with leather at the center and propped up at the crux. The hair on the back of his neck lifted in trepidation

Where the hell was Raina? He searched the faces of each Were. Had they turned her? Had she become a wolf already?

The sound of a muffled struggle reached his ears. Slade shifted position to get a better look. In his impatience his hand slid in the scree, causing small stones to rain down over the rocks. Damn. Double damn.

Dozens of ears swiveled in his direction, and keen eyes searched the rocks. Dark noses sniffed the air, searching for scent.

What the hell are you doing? Achilles asked, clearly irritated by such a basic mistake.

Sorry. I thought I heard Raina.

You did.

"Bring out the Whisperer." The command came from an older, grittier voice Slade hadn't heard in a long time. While he couldn't see the wolf, he could picture him clearly. Silver and huge. The one who had torn his mother to pieces. Loathing and fear shrank his skin to his bones.

Be on alert, here she comes now, Achilles warned.

Slade's body tensed, straining under the pressure of maintaining his flux and the pain building in his stomach from the encroaching moon sickness. Raina, naked